AND SOON COMES THE DARKNESS

An Anthology by

Angelique Archer and J. Mills

Copyright © 2020 by Angelique Archer. All rights reserved.

Cover design © by Onur Burc.

Formatting by Aslam Khan.

No part of this book may be reproduced in any form or by any electronic or mechanical means including information storage and retrieval systems, without permission in writing from the author. The only exception is by a reviewer, who may quote short excerpts in a review.

This book is a work of fiction. Names, characters, places, and incidents either are products of the author's imagination or are used fictitiously. Any resemblance to actual persons, living or dead, events, or locales is entirely coincidental.

Table of Contents

Prologue 3
Chapter 1 5
Chapter 2 15
Chapter 3 27
THE TRACKS IN THE SNOW 37
Prologue 39
Chapter I 43
Chapter II 49
Chapter III 53
Chapter IV 59
Chapter V 63
Chapter VI 69
Chapter VII 75
Chapter VIII 79
Chapter IX 85
Chapter X 91
Epilogue 95
Chapter 4 97
THE TOWN IN THE MOUNTAIN 107
Chapter I 109
Chapter II 119

Chapter III	123
Chapter IV	133
Chapter V	139
Chapter VI	145
Chapter VII	153
Chapter VIII	159
Chapter 5	169
Chapter 6	175
THE VALLEY OF ASH AND SHADOWS	181
Prologue	183
Chapter I	187
Chapter II	195
Chapter III	203
Chapter IV	215
Chapter V	223
Chapter VI	235
Chapter VII	247
Epilogue	259
Chapter 7	263
Chapter 8	269
Chapter 9	277
About the Authors	281

The couple who writes together stays together.

Angelique Archer and J. Mills

Prologue

Cora groaned.

When she furrowed her brows, her skin felt sticky and taut, and an unexpected jolt of pain shot through her head.

Her eyes fluttered open, and she lifted her chin from her chest and tried to look around.

Puzzled, she realized she was sitting in her writing chair in the middle of the living room.

She grunted in confusion. Why wasn't she at her desk, writing like she normally did?

Her mind was fuzzy, but she remembered she needed to write; she had a deadline.

There wasn't time to waste.

Cora attempted to stand, tried to move her arms and legs and make them cooperate.

But she was trapped, immobile.

Icy wind whistled through the cabin, draining it of its warmth, and she shivered. Why was it so cold?

As the fog cleared from her memory, Cora began to put the pieces of the puzzle together, and as she did, her skin prickled. Her gaze drifted to her sides, further and further until she saw the impossibility of her situation.

She was anchored to a chair, her hands tied behind her back.

Someone had done this to her, wanting to hurt her and make her suffer.

Where was he? Had he left?

If so, there was time for her to escape, to get help.

Cora wriggled around fearfully, yanking her wrists against her bindings in an effort to get free.

Hurry! her inner voice screamed. *You don't want to die here!*

The wood floor creaked, and she froze.

"Rise and shine," a steely male voice announced.

Too late.

Not so alone anymore, Cora.

No one will ever hear you scream.

Chapter 1

Cora Parker set the tea kettle back on the stove and turned off the burner. She pulled her auburn hair into a ponytail before reaching in the fridge for the milk, shoving aside several bags of fresh vegetables and cartons of juice until her fingertips brushed against the handle of the plastic gallon jug.

After pouring a little milk into her mug and adding a dollop or two of sugar, she swirled a small spoon around and lifted the cup to her lips as she stared outside.

Snowflakes fluttered gracefully to the ground, finally slowing their descent after a hefty snowfall the night before.

There was at least three feet of snow outside, and Cora was grateful that she'd stocked up on groceries two days prior. She wouldn't have wanted to venture the roads in her rental car now, even if it was all-wheel drive. And it wasn't like they delivered pizza this far away from civilization anyways.

She leaned down to plug in her little Christmas tree that she'd purchased during her grocery run at Walmart, along with a box of cheap ornaments and lights. It was only a couple feet tall, but the warm glow from the twinkling colored lights brought her a modicum of cheer. She fiddled with one of the ornaments that hung from the branches, moving it to a different part of the tree so it was more visible, and she was instantly crushed with a wave of memories from her past.

It was December, almost Christmas, and unlike most people this time of year who were traveling to spend the holidays with loved ones, Cora had opted to isolate herself in her cabin for the next two weeks so that she could finish her latest work-in-progress.

Cora was a writer. And not just any writer, but a *New York Times* bestselling one. Since her late twenties, she'd published over a dozen psychological thrillers, each riddled with more suspense and intrigue than the last.

She didn't start out a writer though. Cora had gone to college for business and marketing and shortly after graduating, landed a job at a major marketing firm in Manhattan.

At first, she was overjoyed, thinking the job would be glamorous and exciting. Maybe even make her parents proud of her, their approval something she'd always sought, but forever seeming elusive and impossible to obtain.

Yet after working there for a few years, she came to the conclusion that she was stuck in a thankless career with long, exhausting hours and unremarkable pay.

And her parents still weren't that proud.

Cora had always found joy in writing. It came naturally to her, the words flying from her fingers effortlessly. It was her escape from an unsavory reality. At night, when she'd get home from the office, she would turn on the television, put on her favorite cozy pajamas, and start typing on the old laptop she still had from college, her mind buzzing with new ideas and storylines.

After working on the first book for over a year, she found an editor, cover artist, and formatter she could afford and self-published her first psychological thriller online.

She distinctly remembered how she felt the first time she received a shipment full of her new book, holding the weight of all of that hard work in her hands, running her fingertips over the smooth matte cover. Emotional. Euphoric. Electric. Each time, that feeling never diminished, no matter how many books she published.

Although the first, and even the second book that followed a year later, didn't bring her much success, just enough royalties to cover groceries and utilities here and there, the next year, she happened to meet a friend of a friend in a publishing press with whom she felt comfortable enough to share her third manuscript.

He quickly recognized her talent and potential and eagerly handed her manuscript to his boss. Within a few months, her third book gained a momentum she wasn't expecting, and Cora was catapulted toward success from there.

She still held onto her marketing job because writing books, albeit their success, didn't seem as reliable or responsible to her. Cora wondered when her luck would run out; it couldn't last forever.

Her biggest fear was that she'd eventually wake up, and her fifteen minutes of fame would be over, forcing her to return to the grueling, mundane existence that was her life before she started pursuing her writing.

But one day on her way to work, something changed, made her second-guess her rationale and let go of her fears. It wasn't a big change, nothing major, nothing cathartic. It was as simple as Cora catching a glimpse of her reflection in the mirror. She touched the thin skin around her eyes, the deep lines forming on her forehead, and brushed down the gray strands popping through her hair.

Cora was in her twenties, too young to feel so old.

The next morning, wondering if she was making the worst, riskiest and simultaneously, most empowering decision of her career, she walked into her boss's office and wordlessly placed a letter of resignation on his desk before turning on her heel and leaving forever.

The years passed, a whirlwind of a decade, and now she had more money than she ever did growing up, two homes, including this cabin in Colorado and a massive seven-bedroom colonial in Virginia, plus a rumored movie deal with Netflix in the works.

Her current work-in-progress was a sequel to her last release, and naturally, the publisher had given her a tight deadline. Not only was Cora under pressure from the publisher, but she had a strong fan base, and they were champing at the bit for the next installment. The outpour of love and support from her fans was wonderful and appreciated, but it also brought with it a good deal of stress.

And nothing killed a writer's groove more than that.

It was the first time in her decade as a writer that Cora wondered if she could get this book done in such a short turn-around.

Of course, it wasn't just the anxiety that was slaughtering her progress.

Oddly enough, the more successful she was, the less inspired she became. She struggled to find a muse, a plot, an idea that would give birth to a novel that would land a bestseller list. That was the easier part.

Then she had to weave the story together, make sure there were no holes, that the twists and turns of the plot made sense. More times than she cared to count, Cora had ended up with a tangled mess of a storyline, one that neither she nor her editor could make sense of, and unraveling it was as challenging as finally getting around to untangling the necklaces in her jewelry box that had been sitting like that on her dresser for years.

Cora shuddered. Untangling necklaces was probably her least favorite activity; watching paint dry honestly sounded like more fun.

And when she found herself trying to conquer such gargantuan writing hurdles, Cora couldn't focus on much else. She was a worker bee. Sometimes she would be so deeply engrossed in her work that she'd forget to eat. It happened so often that she had resorted to setting alarms on her phone as a reminder.

Breakfast? Check.

Lunch? Whoops, forgot that one.

Dinner? Yeah... better eat, or you'll die.

But at the end of the day, it didn't matter if she remembered to eat, if she managed to sit down at her desk and painstakingly type a few words...

Since when did a few pathetic words on the page count as a victory for the day?

There had been a time when she could easily write ten thousand words in one sitting.

Cora fearfully wondered what happened to the creative inspiration that at one point had made her a bestseller, that in the past had so readily flowed from a well with no bottom.

Maybe your well's run dry.

Maybe you just don't have any good ideas left.

Words of encouragement like this from her inner monologue made Cora want to crawl under the bed sheets and hide from the world.

She took a long, contemplative sip of her tea and gazed into the wide swath of trees beyond the window, her cabin perched high in the snow-capped mountains.

At first, the home was merely a retreat to escape the hustle and bustle of the city, the isolation a welcome reprieve. What started as a trip a couple times a year to write without distractions was becoming more and more frequent, to the point that Cora was considering selling her Virginia estate. It wasn't like she had anyone to share it with anyways.

Instead, each time she ventured to the cabin to write, she ended up staying a little longer than she intended. And each time she went, she lost contact a little bit more with the rest of the world. She became a little sadder, a little more reclusive. She stayed in the same worn cardigan and sweatpants and didn't bother washing her hair half as often as she should.

She simply didn't care. Cora had everything she needed here.

The cabin was modestly sized, only two bedrooms and a simple living area, probably a thousand square feet at best. And it was cozy. She'd had it professionally decorated by an interior designer before she moved in, personalized touches throughout, including plush rugs her toes sank into, paintings of soothing forest scenes on the polished wood walls, unique décor such as a World War II-era typewriter and an antique ink pen and ink pot set from England which sat on a bookshelf crammed with her books and books from her favorite authors... everything that amounted to an ideal writer's haven.

Cora had no husband, no children. She had no family anymore. She was very much alone.

You have no one to blame for that but yourself.

It was true. She'd chosen to prioritize her writing above all else. Her choice.

But what did it cost you?

And at what cost did you maintain your success?

At what cost, Cora?

At. What. Cost?

She shook her head. Enough with the nonsense. She needed to write. Less than two weeks remained before she had to submit her manuscript to her publisher.

Cora cinched her fluffy robe tightly around her narrowing waist and sat down at her desk which faced another window featuring panoramic views of the mountains flanking her on either side. The sun was high in the sky, its bright beams reflecting off the snow. She cracked her knuckles and opened her computer screen.

Her fingers hovered over the keyboard, and she took another look at the mediocre, waifish outline printed out beside the computer.

She was just about to start typing when her phone alarm went off, reminding her to eat lunch. She shut off the alarm and silenced her phone, determined to crank out five thousand words before dinnertime.

Cora typed away for hours then paused to read what she'd written, checking to make sure it fit in with the rest of the story.

To her dismay, she found her writing uninspired and poorly written. Not even caring to see if there was anything to salvage from what she'd just done, she highlighted page after page of work and, without a second thought, hit "Delete."

With a sigh of frustration, Cora stood up and walked to the kitchen. She'd purchased several bottles of wine at the grocery store. Maybe it was time to open one now.

Hey, it's five o'clock somewhere.

Actually, it was already past five. She'd completely skipped lunch.

She uncorked a bottle of Merlot and dumped the now-cold tea stagnating in her mug into the sink, feeling too lazy to get one of the wine glasses from the cabinet. She filled the mug close to the rim then opened the fridge, her stomach growling loudly.

After pulling out a package of chicken breasts and bags of assorted fresh vegetables, Cora rinsed everything and then placed it all on two cutting boards. She reached for one of the serrated knives from the knife block and started chopping.

The sun was setting, fiery orange rays slowly sinking lower and lower beneath the horizon, until it disappeared completely.

When she was finished cooking, Cora added some rice to her plate and topped it with the sesame seasoned chicken and vegetables. It was one of her favorite comfort food meals.

She returned to her desk and took a deep breath. If she wrote for the next six hours, she could still make her writing goal for the day. She scrolled through the previous pages, spearing a piece of chicken with her fork while she read.

Then she stopped mid-bite.

Something had quickly passed by the window near the front door.

A flash of darkness.

A tall shadow.

Either her imagination was running wild as she wrote or…

Or she was no longer alone.

Chapter 2

Goosebumps broke out all along Cora's skin, and her heart started thrumming louder and louder in her chest.

Immediately, she rose to her feet and walked to the window, pushing aside the curtains. The moonlight pulsated through the tall pines, casting long, spindly shadows onto the blank canvas of untouched snow below.

She craned her neck, squinting to see what was on either side of the window.

After what seemed like an eternity of heightened tension in the still quiet, a deer made its way past the front porch.

Cora exhaled in relief and rubbed her forehead. She was tired and worn out, and now her mind was playing tricks on her.

"Calm down, Cora. It was nothing," she said aloud, chastising herself for her stupidity. The sound of her voice filling the emptiness was oddly comforting, and she wished she had a television or radio, anything to keep the silence from taking over once more.

The cabin was devoid of these distractions, the intention being that she could work on her books without movies and television shows vying for her attention. But maybe the next time she was in town, she would allow herself a small luxury and pick up a television.

The wind rushed through the trees, the glass panes of the window shuddering from the gusts that pelted it, while low-hanging branches scraped across the roof of the cabin. In moments like these, Cora was reminded of how alone she really was in the mountains.

You're too old for scary stories. You're perfectly safe out here.

Maybe you should start writing romance. Your own books are getting to you.

She made her way back to her desk and took another sip of wine, noticing for the first time that she'd finished more than half the bottle.

It was the alcohol. It had to be the alcohol.

With a reassured chuckle, she went back to her manuscript, eating while she read.

For whatever reason, she actually began to see progress in her work as she steadily clicked away on the keyboard. There was certainly an element of spookiness revealing itself out of nowhere from the plot, but she liked where it was headed and kept writing, not caring that it was already late or that she was exhausted.

Her glasses were low on her nose, hair thrown messily into a bun on top of her head, her mouth set in a grim line of determination. It was while her fingers danced along the keys, so quickly there were almost sparks spewing forth from her fingertips, when she heard two loud creaks from the deck in the back.

Heavy creaks.

Like footsteps.

Cora remembered how she had drawn the curtains back earlier… and how she'd forgotten to close them.

This left her feeling very vulnerable and exposed.

An eerie sensation washed over her.

She felt them. Eyes. Eyes fixated on her. Eyes burning with anticipation.

Was she being watched?

Cora didn't want to check. She was afraid of what she might find, but as if she had no control of her own movements, she cautiously looked over her shoulder, inch by inch, mentally preparing herself for something horrible.

But when she faced the sliding glass door, all she saw was her own reflection.

She jumped to her feet, her legs almost giving out after being bent beneath her on the chair for so long, and rushed to the back to shut the curtains.

Stop it. You're doing it again.

There's nothing out there. It's just the wind or a wild animal.

Keep writing! You're finally going to make your wordcount.

She backed away from the glass and shivered, wrapping her arms around her waist.

Maybe she would have felt better if she had an alarm system.

Or a gun.

You don't even know how to shoot a gun.

There is NOTHING out there.

Cora reluctantly sat back down.

And that was when she saw it. The doorknob on the front door was turning.

Slowly.

Right, then left.

Left, then right.

Paralyzed, her blood ran cold.

She wasn't imagining it. Someone was at her door.

Cora did the first thing she could think of and ran to

the wall to switch off the lights.

Then she stumbled over to the desk, crouched low, and grabbed her phone, sandwiching herself between the sofa and the wall and hastily dialing 9-1-1. But to her utter dismay, the little bar of reception in the left-hand corner flickered on and off and then disappeared entirely, replaced with the dreaded "No Service." The reception was never good in the mountains, but she had yet to have none at all. Perhaps the storm the night before had knocked out the tower.

She peeked over the arm of the sofa, noticing the doorknob had stopped turning. Although she was frightened of what awaited, Cora had to know what was out there. The morbid curiosity made it impossible for her to stay still. She crawled over to the closest window and millimeter by millimeter, nudged the curtain aside.

There were footprints in the snow running along the front porch.

Large, deep outlines of shoes that were unmistakable.

Calm down.

Cora heard the small panes of glass on the door shatter and clank to the floor. She darted over to the kitchen and grabbed one of the knives from her knife block and edged backward into the living room, her eyes widening in horror as a gloved hand reached through the broken shards and began groping for the doorknob.

She knew she only had moments before the intruder would be standing inside her house.

You have to go outside, go back down the mountain. Call for help.

Cora took one last look at the hand just before it grasped the doorknob to unlock it. Without a second thought, she fled to the sliding glass door leading to the back deck. She violently yanked it open, but every few inches, the heavy door would catch on the metal tracks, forcing her to pull harder in desperation while she stared at the front door as it slowly opened.

With a final heave, the door jostled back enough to allow her to slip through. Once outside, Cora inhaled sharply when harsh, icy air blasted her body, her robe and pajamas ill-fitted to protect her from the bitter cold.

She whirled around and saw a tall, dark figure move through the front door. Terrified, Cora spun away from the cabin and toward the trees.

But if she wasn't prepared for the cold that greeted her moments before, her bare feet were even less ready as she clumsily stumbled through the thick snow coating the mountain. As soft as it was, the snow burned the soles of her feet, mushing in between her toes, and up around her ankles and shins.

Cora ducked behind a tree, pausing to lean against the trunk as she lifted one foot at a time to give it a momentary reprieve from the pain.

She looked down the mountain, realizing she had so much further to go before she got to the main road.

In the distance, the flickering sign for the gas station where she had filled up her rental car after picking up groceries now seemed galaxies away, a little speck of light nearly lost amidst a backdrop of pine trees and winding roads, the only piece of civilization between her and the town below.

She groaned and rubbed her feet, trying to get the blood flowing again. They hurt so much.

She wouldn't make it far. Not without shoes and the proper clothes.

You have to go back.

Her car was sitting inside the garage. If she could get to it without being seen, she could drive down the mountain and get help.

She pawed at the pockets on her robe, then remembered that the house keys were in her bedroom on her dresser where she always left them.

Cora, you idiot. Of course they're inside. Who carries their car keys in their house robe?

Her feet and hands growing numb, she glanced back at the house.

Maybe he's gone. He was just a thief. He took what he wanted and left.

Cora dug her fingernails into the rough bark of the pine tree, her body shaking uncontrollably.

Could she risk it?

She looked over her shoulder, back down the mountain. Her teeth were clattering together loudly, and she could feel herself growing drowsy.

In sub-zero temperatures, she wouldn't survive if she stayed outside much longer. Hypothermia would set in, and she'd be dead before she even made it to the bottom of the mountain, much less the nearest town.

You don't have a choice. Either you go back, or you die.

Her eyes filled with tears, but they froze as they trickled down her cheeks.

She turned back to the cabin and cautiously made her way from one tree to the next, using the trunks as cover.

The cabin seemed deceptively cozy as she approached it, warm light filtering through the curtains. The intruder must have turned the lights back on to see what he could steal.

Cora cursed him under her breath.

How long has it been? Did you give him enough time to take what he wanted and get out?

You can't wait any longer. You can't.

She swayed closer to the cabin until she was standing a few feet from the porch.

The front door was slightly ajar. Cora stared at it long and hard, trying to focus. Her mind grew fuzzy, the freezing temperature sending her into delirium.

She wondered if she was going crazy, envisaging an intruder had broken into her home, when it was nothing more than her imagination getting the best of her.

Taking tentative steps forward, she found herself standing at the entrance of the cabin.

Her feet were completely numb; she didn't notice that there were shards of glass beneath them, cutting into her frozen flesh.

She edged the door open a bit further and stood there, holding the knife out in front of her, at war with herself.

Am I losing my mind?

The sound of a cabinet drawer being slammed shut deeper in the cabin answered the question for her.

No. No, you are not.

The direness of her situation snapped her out of her stupor, and she stumbled backward, falling down the steps of the porch, but quickly springing back to her feet and running for cover at the side of the house.

Bloody footsteps trailed behind her, but Cora didn't have time to examine her wounds.

She smashed her body against the wood siding.

Where is he?

Clenching her jaw so that her teeth would stop clattering, Cora leaned over to a window and tried to see through the slit in the curtains.

A tall, thin man dressed in black from head to toe had his back to her.

Cora gasped and crouched under the window.

Yes, there's a bad guy in your house. You don't have time to be surprised.

She had to get those keys. Short of having the upper hand on him with the element of surprise and winning a knife fight she obviously wasn't trained for, there was no other option.

Maybe she could sneak in through another window.

Cora tried to recollect which, if any, might be open.

Then she remembered leaving the bathroom window cracked just a sliver. It was an old habit she had done in every house she'd ever lived in, to keep fresh air circulating.

She stood and darted around the side of the cabin until she reached the bathroom.

Her fingers, bright red, pried the window open as stealthily as possible. But the window was high, perhaps too high, for her to be able to hoist herself up and through it.

Cora searched around and found a large ceramic potted plant, one that, judging from its brittle, shriveled branches, had been forgotten a long time ago. She flipped the planter over and carefully climbed on top.

Heaving her body over the metal ledge and wriggling her shoulders through the small space, Cora finally freed herself and ungracefully tumbled onto the plush bathmat below.

She clung to the edge of the bathtub, waiting for the intruder to run in and find her.

But after a minute and the constant sound of cabinets closing and objects being moved around, Cora concluded he hadn't heard her.

She looked at her feet and hands, how they were swollen and red. She flexed them a little, prickliness the only sensation she could feel as she warmed.

It's okay. You're alive.

Now get those keys.

She rose on unsteady legs and quietly made her way into the bedroom. As silently as she could manage, Cora began to close the bedroom door leading into the living room. She could see the man still rifling through the contents in the drawers.

After flipping the flimsy lock on the cheap gold doorknob, she took a chair from beside her dresser and jammed it under the doorknob.

You're doing great. He doesn't know you're here.

Cora backed up until her legs hit the bedframe, and she waited there, her chest heaving, expecting the stranger to burst through the door at any second.

Yet there was nothing but silence, painful, dreadful, ominous silence.

Then she heard a creak from behind her, from the closet.

Cora stopped breathing, and her eyes looked to her periphery.

The last thing she thought before she blacked out was that she had been wrong this whole time.

There were two of them.

Chapter 3

"Rise and shine."

Cora stiffened in her chair, suddenly alert. All at once, she remembered what had happened, how two intruders had interrupted her quiet mountain retreat, violating the safe space of her snowed-in domicile, her private sanctuary.

As her vision sharpened, a man came into view, dressed completely in black. He was tall and thin, dressed in a thick parka, a hood pulled low over his face, almost obscuring his features.

"She's awake," he called out.

"Shit. Knock her out again," a female answered from another room.

"Please," Cora managed. "Don't hurt me."

The man knelt down, still several feet away from her. He sighed. "Hurting you was never part of the plan. You weren't even supposed to be here."

She looked at him with wide, pleading eyes. "Then let me go."

He shook his head.

Cora chewed on the inside of her cheek, a nervous habit. She wanted to ask him, but she was afraid of the answer.

Just ask. What do you have to lose at this point?

"What are you going to do to me?"

He responded more quickly than she'd expected, showing her he had considered the various possibilities of her fate. "I don't know. If I cut you loose, you'll go to the police."

"No, I won't. I promise."

He grunted.

A woman appeared from the bedroom. "What the hell are you doing? We don't have time for this." In one of her hands was a black duffel bag while the other held a gold locket Cora had left on her nightstand.

Unlike the man, his companion wasn't wearing a hoodie. She had a beanie drawn over her head, long, dark hair swept into a low ponytail. Her eyes were light blue, a stark contrast against her raven hair and pale skin. She might have been beautiful once, but over time, her features had become harsh and pointy, and the glint in her eyes failed to hide a palpable cruelty.

"I told you someone was home, but *you* wanted to risk it, and now this bitch has seen our faces," the woman shouted as she turned and stormed back into Cora's bedroom.

You're in deep shit.

Cora searched the room in desperation, her gaze settling on her cell phone which was now located on the kitchen counter.

That's it.

She so rarely received calls from anyone outside of her agent, and he knew she was holed up in her cabin, diligently working to finish her next bestseller. To make sure she was on track with her deadlines, he rang her every night, and she never missed one of his calls. If Cora didn't answer tonight, he would certainly sense something was wrong and send the police to check on her.

It was a shot in the dark, the only glimmer of hope she could hold onto for now.

Until then, she needed time.

Cora's eyes met Damon's. "Please. I'll give you whatever you want. I have money. And a safe," she blurted. But her face blanched when she realized she'd said too much.

When she'd promised something she shouldn't have.

She was aware of this, somewhere in the deepest

recesses of her mind, the part of her mind that wasn't focused on her survival.

The man cocked his head, pushing back his hood in interest. He had dark hair and similar features as the woman, but his gray eyes remained stoic and his expression measured and calm. "A safe? Where is it?"

"I... I can't tell you," Cora replied sheepishly, lowering her head.

"Where?" he reiterated.

She said nothing and stared at the ground, listening to the woman tear apart her room looking for valuables.

"Look," the man began, interrupting her thoughts. He cast a quick look over his shoulder and lowered his voice. "You need to tell me where it is. My sister..." He leaned in ever so slightly, as if he was going to confide in her. "She isn't as... understanding."

Sister.

So this was a brother-sister job.

To Cora, he sounded genuine, almost as if he was pleading with her to let him help her so his sister couldn't force him to do something he clearly didn't want to do.

But before she could respond, his sister stomped back in. "Did you not hear me the first time?"

She glared at Cora, then back at her brother. "Are you *talking* to her?" she barked incredulously.

The man looked at his hands, refusing to make eye contact with her. Although he dwarfed her in size, his body language made it almost seem as though he was… afraid?

"Marisa… I was just trying to figure out where she kept her money."

The woman reared her hand back and slapped him hard. "You dumbass. Now she knows my name. No wonder dad never respected you. You couldn't find your way out of a paper bag." She gestured around them. "She's a big shot writer. There are only so many places to hide money in this cabin. If you don't start helping me search for it, I'm just going to off the two of you for wasting my time."

Both Cora and the man gaped at her. "You need to calm down. You know how shit goes down when you get overly emotional," the man chastised.

"Oh, spare me the high and mighty, *Damon*. You're just as rotten as me." She rested a hand on her hip smugly. "Now she knows both our names. If we get caught, you're going down with me, little brother."

Cora watched as Damon reluctantly went over to examine the shelves in the living room, shaking his head in disapproval. When Marisa was satisfied that he was actually going to help her, she retreated back into the bedroom.

Damon and Marisa.

His gloved fingers slid across the bookshelves, then rubbed the dust between his thumb and forefinger. He paused in front of the shelf that held all of her published books. Pulling one out, he scanned the front cover, then began reading the back.

Cora studied him from the corner of her eye, noticing that as he continued to read, his eyebrows would subtly raise with interest.

"You write thrillers?"

She nodded slowly. "Mostly."

He returned the book to the shelf, then took out another. "I like horror. But I don't read much. I like movies better. Ever done any movies?"

"Not yet. But my agent says there's rumor of a Netflix deal with one of my series."

"You've got to be making good money then. Or you will be," he mused.

"Maybe."

"It must be nice, being rich. Being able to afford whatever you want. Go wherever you feel like going."

Cora detected the slightest bit of vitriol, or maybe jealousy, in his tone. She nodded. "I've worked hard to get to where I am."

Damon's face shot up from reading. "So you're saying if you don't have money, you aren't working hard enough?"

Cora shook her head quickly. "No," she backpedaled. The last thing she wanted to do was anger him. "I'm just saying I've worked hard to be successful." She thought for a moment. "And I'm not even that successful, not like Stephen King or anyone."

"We've always been poor. No matter how hard we worked, we couldn't seem to get out of this shit town."

Cora was unsure why he was sharing all of this with her. But she stayed silent and allowed him to continue nonetheless.

"If you would have asked me ten, twenty years ago if this is what I saw myself doing, breaking into houses and stealing from people, I would have been disgusted. I was a good kid growing up. I always tried to do what I was told. I studied hard in school. I had plans." Damon hung his head a little. "I used to want to open a restaurant with my mom when I was younger. We'd cook together every night, nothing fancy, but I liked it. It was our thing." He snapped from his reverie. "But you just keep getting dealt shit card after shit card, and one day you snap."

She didn't know if he wanted her to interject or offer some type of encouragement. "So I guess I'm not your first then."

He tilted his head to the side slightly, perplexed at first by her quip, then ignored it. "Anyways, all that's to say people like me didn't dream of the life we have. Or what we're doing to you right now."

Instead of putting the book back, he held onto it and went to sit in front of her on the sofa.

He folded his hands on either side of the book, pensively staring at it for an uncomfortably long time, before he finally looked up at her.

"I tell you what…" he said quietly. "If you can tell me a good horror story, and," his voice got even quieter, "give me the code to that safe, I might just let you go."

Hope suddenly surged in Cora's heart. There was a chance she might live to see another day. But Marisa… "Your sister wouldn't let that happen. She wants to kill me."

He shook his head. "She'll be searching that room for a while, thinking there's some kind of treasure stowed away in there waiting to be discovered. This is just between you and I. My sister doesn't have to know. I'll say you escaped."

Cora's mind raced as she struggled to find story material when her life was on the line. Horror. He wanted to hear something scary.

She looked outside at the snow falling on the ground, the lights from her tiny Christmas tree sparkling in the reflection of the sliding glass door.

You can do this.

You're a writer. Storytelling is your thing.

Think, think, think.

Appeal to his empathy; make the story relatable.

"What happens if you hate it?" she asked hesitantly.

"Is it scary?"

"I'll try."

He frowned. "Trying isn't going to get you out of here."

The harsh reality of his words hung heavily in the air.

"Okay," she breathed, an idea starting to formulate.

With one last look over his shoulder, Damon set the book on the coffee table and settled back into the couch. He gestured widely. "Whenever you're ready."

THE TRACKS IN THE SNOW

Prologue

THE TRACKS IN THE SNOW

Cherryton, San Bordelo Mountain Pass

In spite of Walt Ackerman's windshield wipers furiously shifting back and forth on the old cherry picker, the snow was piling up so quickly on the glass that he couldn't really see more than a few feet in front of him.

"What the hell kind of company sends a man out on Christmas morning?" he grumbled angrily, his eyes narrowed to slits as he tried to navigate through the snow.

The power had gone out in Cherryton and a few of the other neighboring towns, and they wanted him to go and fix it.

Most of the other electrical linemen were away for the holidays this year, just his luck. He was one of three men who were still local, and he happened to draw the shortest proverbial straw, being less senior than the other two.

Walt had just started opening gifts with his wife and children when he got the call about the downed power line. The timing couldn't have been worse. He and his wife had finally purchased the shiny black bike his son had been begging for over the last eight months, and the boy's hands were tearing at the awkwardly wrapped Christmas paper when his work phone started to ring.

It wasn't one of those calls he could ignore or send to voicemail like he did all the time with his pestering mother-in-law. His boss was on the phone, with orders from his boss that people could not be without power for Christmas.

He slowed the truck when he finally spotted it. One telephone pole was resting at an angle, while the one beside it had completely fallen, taking down several power lines with it. Thick black cables dangled precariously from the slanted pole.

Walt groaned. It was much worse than he'd imagined. He wouldn't be able to fix this by himself.

Knowing his boss would be angry if he left without providing some kind of damage report, Walt sighed and parked the truck as close as he safely could to the downed lines. He pulled on another jacket, his ski mask, and some heavy gloves and climbed out of the truck. After he was in the bucket, he pressed the remote to ascend until he was eye-level with the pole and could see everything else beneath him.

The damage was bad. And it wasn't just the two poles and fallen lines. A few poles down the road showed the same misfortune.

Walt frowned as he surveyed the disrepair.

There weren't any downed trees, any sign that the poles had been knocked over from the snowstorm.

What had brought them down if it wasn't the weather?

Yanking off his right glove with a grimace, Walt snapped photos of the damage with his phone as best he could, the battery nearly empty as the frigid temperatures sucked the life from it, but the images were difficult to see, blurred with the flurry of snow flying past.

Walt scrolled through them hastily, hoping there were a few clear ones so his boss could make out the damage and needed repairs. But an image in one of the photos caught his eye, and he swiped backward to look again.

Wiping at the screen in frustration, he peered closer. There was something out of place in one particular photo that wasn't in the others.

A giant white blur near the edge of the forest beyond him.

He zoomed in. It looked like it could just be a cluster of snowflakes obscuring part of the lens.

But as the image grew larger, the hairs on the back of Walt's neck stood up.

The picture wasn't blurry because of snowflakes, as he'd originally thought.

No, it was unfocused because a figure was moving

rapidly past when he snapped the photo.

A monstrous form, beastly and gargantuan in its size and shape.

Walt kept zooming in, beginning to make out the details. Pale fur, gnarled horns...

The truck rattled under him, and the phone slipped from his fingers. He grabbed the rim of the bucket with both hands to steady himself, preparing to lean over the side, trying to see where the phone fell so he could retrieve it.

He was about to look over the edge when the cherry picker violently shook. His eyes widened just in time to see a massive hand with razor-sharp claws swinging toward his face, and before he could gasp in protest, his head was flying through the air, an arc of blood in its wake. It tumbled to the ground, rolling and rolling, until it disappeared beneath the truck.

Chapter I

THE TRACKS IN THE SNOW

"Amber, look! The train's pulling up!" Nine year-old Cameron "Cam" Danvers called out to his sister, pushing the glasses up on his freckled nose and closing the book he was reading. He rose to his feet from the bench he was sitting on and stood on his tiptoes to peer down the lracks as the train rounded the bend.

Fourteen year-old Amber looked up from her phone for barely a second, wavy blonde hair falling back from her face, before she slumped her cheek against her hand and buried her face in her phone again.

Cam sighed and sat back down beside her, flipping open his book once more even though he was already bored from reading it; soon it would be too dark to see the pages. Besides, he would have plenty of time on the train to finish it. They had a solid five-hour train ride through the mountains until they made it home to their parents'.

He didn't have anything else to do anyways. It wasn't like his sister was going to hang out with him. He missed those days, when they were each other's best friend. He wondered what happened to that girl. The days where they'd spend sunrise to sunset playing in their backyard, their imaginations running wild with make-believe adventures, seemed to be over.

Amber was physically there beside him, but it was almost as if she wasn't. Since she became a teenager, and his parents bought her a phone, she had changed. She'd lost interest in being his big sister, in being one of his only friends.

Snow began to fall, slow at first, then faster and faster.

He dog-eared the page he was on and stared at the snowflakes as they swirled around and blanketed the ground. Cam was hoping this Christmas, he'd get some time with Amber since she wouldn't have her friends, her laptop, or much reception at their grandparents'. He wasn't trying to be greedy; he just wanted his sister all to himself. But as soon as they got there, he was crushed to find out that her phone *did* in fact work, and true to form, she was glued to it like she always was. She didn't want to go sledding; she didn't want to make a snowman; and she wasn't interested in baking Christmas cookies.

Little by little, Cam was learning to accept this new reality.

Whether it was his sister or his parents, Cam felt like no one wanted to spend time with him anymore, and while his grandparents tried their best to do fun things with them, Cam did not like the idea of spending Christmas without their mom and dad. It just wasn't the same without them, and he fervently hoped this would be the first and last time it ever happened.

Jillian and Peter Danvers both had the misfortune of having to work Christmas this year, each of them high-powered corporate attorneys at the same firm working a complex case that was slated to go before the judge on the second of January. Their grandparents, not wanting the children to miss out on Christmas morning and all the festivities leading up to it, insisted they come out to visit them a few days before Christmas, and then they could take the train back to Piedmont and spend the last vestiges of Christmas Day with their parents. Cam knew his parents felt guilty about missing Christmas with their children, and he tried to be understanding and mature about it. But this type of thing was becoming more and more of a habit now that they were some of the most senior attorneys at the firm, promotions which came with their own sizeable responsibilities and obligations that meant more hours in the office and fewer hours at home.

So here the children were, waiting in near-darkness for a train that would take them back to the city, to a lifestyle that Cam was becoming less and less fond of because he was becoming more and more invisible to everyone around him.

The train rolled to a stop in front of them, and Cam nudged his sister with his foot then stood and grabbed his superhero-themed duffel bag.

He studied the bag for a moment, then looked up at Amber. Maybe if he seemed more grown-up, she would want to spend time with him again because she would view him more as an equal rather than a pesky little brother. His heart sank as he ran his fingers over the Marvel characters, deciding he would get rid of the bag when he got home.

"Which seats did we get?" Amber asked him, finally pocketing her phone as she pulled her bright pink mittens over her hands.

Cam pulled the tickets from his pocket. "Car seven, seats ten and eleven," he replied. Seeing that he had her attention, he continued, "Hey, we should explore the other cars once we put our stuff away."

Amber seemed less than enthused. "You can. I'll watch our bags."

They started to climb the steps of the train once the other passengers disembarked.

Frustrated with himself for offering such a lame suggestion, Cam frowned. Was it actually that lame? They would have done that before. But cool kids had better things to do than explore trains. Then his expression brightened when he remembered what his grandma had packed away for them. "Are you hungry? Grandma made us some awesome snacks. She put a ton of those cookies in there for us."

She trudged ahead of him, carefully making her way

past the many rows of seats until she found theirs. After she tossed her bag into the compartment above their heads, helping him do the same with his bag, she slouched into the worn seat and pulled out her phone once more. "You can have mine. I ate way too many this weekend. I don't want to get fat."

Cam felt the tears burn in his eyes. He pulled out his asthma inhaler and sprayed it while taking a deep breath. He knew he shouldn't be upset over this, but deep down, he wondered if he and Amber would ever have a reason to hang out again, or if the next three years before she left for college would go by, and they would be no more than ghosts living in the same house.

Chapter II

THE TRACKS IN THE SNOW

Amber unlocked her phone, subconsciously needing to check her newsfeed for the second time in the last ten minutes. It was almost as though her fingertips automatically knew where to tap on the screen, opening those notoriously familiar apps, like muscle memory. She was bored, and the urge to mindlessly entertain herself on social media was too tempting to resist.

For the next twenty minutes, she scrolled through her phone robotically, her eyes glazed over as she scanned past the photos of her friends. She saw countless pictures of her girlfriends sharing photos of their Christmas celebrations, smiling brightly, their outfits stylish, their hair perfectly sleek and straight.

She ran her fingers through her hair self-consciously, trying to detangle the knots that had ensnared themselves in her blonde locks, so that she would be photo-ready.

Smile. Look like you're having fun.

Milliseconds before she snapped the selfie, Cam

popped into the photo with her, opening his mouth wide and making a ridiculously silly face.

As she compulsively went back to check it, she groaned.

"Ugh, Cam. You ruined it."

He leaned in to look at it with her. "Keep it! I like it!"

She rolled her eyes. "No, I'm not posting this. I'm cropping you out." His face fell, and he suddenly looked like the saddest kid in the world.

He turned away from her and looked out the window again.

She saw this and paused before finalizing the cropped version of the picture. And then, as if she changed her mind, reverted the photo back to the version with her brother still in it and started to upload the picture to her profile. Amber waited impatiently while the blue download bar moved incrementally, then stopped moving altogether.

She glowered at the screen petulantly, knowing as long as they were in the mountains suffering through this snowstorm, the photo would never load.

Her friends would have all of these phenomenal pictures where they looked happy and were having fun, and she was stuck for the next five hours on a train.

Amber settled back in her seat, resting her head against

the shabby material. She knew her frustration was absurd and misplaced. Why was she so obsessed to see what her friends were doing every minute of every day? Seeing what they wore, what they did, what they ate? Why did any of it matter?

The train lurched slightly as it slithered along the tracks like a giant silver serpent, and Amber turned to Cam. His face was inches from the glass as he stared out the window, captivated by the snow as it blew over the train.

Her stomach growled, and he looked up at her. He reached into his backpack and pulled out one of their grandmother's freshly baked cookies, offering it up to her.

"Cookie?" he asked.

She took it from him. "Thanks."

"Want to get some real food? There's a food car a few cars down."

His blue eyes were big and hopeful, and even though Amber didn't feel like getting up and was still annoyed that her picture never loaded, she knew her brother needed more than just sugar in his system.

"Yeah, I guess."

His face lit up like a firefly at this.

She shouldered her pink purse and got up. Cam led the way, happily swinging between the seats every so often and looking back at her with a huge smile on his face. She hadn't seen him this excited in a long time.

"Try it!" he exclaimed. "It's fun!"

She pushed her hair behind her ear and quickly looked around in embarrassment. "Not a chance."

But even though she was way too grown-up to do the same thing, seeing him so happy was infectious, and in spite of herself, she smiled, too.

Chapter III

THE TRACKS IN THE SNOW

The dining car was lined on both sides with small two- and four-person tables covered in red and green polyester tablecloths and adorned with fake holly berries in little glass vases.

There were big windows that allowed passengers to see more of the outdoors while they ate, but since it was now dark outside, thin panels of lights running along the ceiling illuminated the car.

Only two people were there, a young cashier standing behind the counter and a man in his mid-thirties with curly, unruly brown hair, thin lips, and glasses sitting low on the bridge of his nose. He was avidly chatting with the cashier who didn't really seem to be following what he was saying, but still nodded politely all the same.

Cam ran up to the counter and began browsing the sandwiches and snacks on display.

"I want a pretzel with nacho cheese dipping sauce."

Amber's stomach rumbled again. "I think I'll have one

of those pizzas," she replied. "We should get some Sour Patch Kids, too."

Cam grinned. Some of his favorite memories were the nights he and Amber spent alone, where their parents would leave them money for a pizza, and they'd walk to the nearest gas station and pick up all the candy they could buy with the leftover change from the pizza.

After they placed their orders with the cashier, Cam wandered the rest of the car while Amber waited for their food at a table.

The train wasn't moving quickly, and Amber watched the scenery pass by, admiring how it looked like everything was coated in a thick blanket of snow, how the giant evergreen trees seemed more majestic with their branches dipped in white.

But she wanted to admire everything from the safe, warm confines of the train. The forest beyond the trees looked bone-chilling, unwelcoming... haunting... a never-ending ocean of snow that could easily swallow up two kids.

Something large and pale darted through the pines, running parallel to the train. She jerked back in surprise. Whatever it was had been gigantic and impossibly fast. She mashed her hands against the window, trying to find it once more.

"The seismic activity in that area had been unprecedented. We'd never seen anything like it before.

And so I flew down from Utah last week, trying to figure out what caused it," Amber vaguely registered the stranger saying to the cashier, but she couldn't tear her eyes away from the forest.

"'Seismic activity?'" her brother piped up, his voice laced with interest.

"Yes, seismic…" The man looked down, remembering he was speaking to a child. He then lifted his hands, pressing them together, side by side. "We live on these plates that, over the span of millions of years, move around like this," he explained, shifting his hands back and forth.

Cam seemed eager to hear more, which was unusual for the scientist. He was accustomed to people's eyes glazing over whenever he talked about his job. So even though he was talking to a kid, the thought of someone actually being interested in what he did for a living reinvigorated the excitement he had for his job. "You see, sometimes the plates want to move, but they can't because they're held against each other." The man squeezed his middle finger and thumb together. "Once the pressure releases," he told the boy, suddenly snapping his fingers, "*that's* the perfect storm for an earthquake."

After a second of quiet contemplation, Cam asked, "So is that what you were doing here, studying earthquakes?"

"Well, my young friend, that's funny you'd ask. All of our equipment is telling us there has been earthquake-like activity in and around these mountain towns, but there are *no* fault lines. So it's like having a snap without the fingers."

"But you didn't find anything?" Cam inquired.

"Ultimately, no," the man responded dejectedly. It was a bitter reminder that he'd spent many sleepless hours and months of painstaking research leading up to his trip trying to solve a scientific mystery that, at the current juncture, seemed to have no answer.

"Maybe it wasn't something natural. Maybe it was something you haven't seen before. From another world. Monsters."

Monsters.

Amber thought about what she had seen in the trees. A polar bear perhaps? How silly for her to think it was anything else.

Then she whirled around in her chair. "Cam, come here. Don't talk to strangers."

"Thanks for telling me about your earthquakes," Cam said to the man with a wave, before making his way back to his sister.

"Thanks for listening," the man answered in earnest.

When Cam noticed Amber's eyes were fixated on something unseen outside, his gaze shifted from her to the window and back to her again. "What are you looking at?"

Amber struggled to decipher what she'd seen. "I... I don't know. I thought I saw something." She shook her head. "But it was probably nothing."

The train suddenly slowed until it came to an unexpected stop.

Everyone in the dining car looked at one another. Amber twisted in her seat, her blonde waves tumbling over her shoulder.

The doors slid open, and the conductor appeared. Both siblings instinctively rose to their feet.

"Please stay in your seats," the conductor told them, gesturing with his hands for them to sit back down.

"What's going on?" Cam asked. "Why did we stop?"

The conductor seemed annoyed with him and gave a subtle eyeroll. "Stay in your seats. There's an obstruction on the tracks, but don't worry. We have people currently working out there to clear the issue. What we need from everyone is to stay put for now."

Once the conductor had moved on to the next car, Cam turned to Amber impishly, the opportunity for an adventure together too overwhelming to resist. "Let's go see what it is!"

Amber looked down at him. "Are you crazy? It's freezing cold out there. And you heard what that guy said. We're supposed to stay in our seats."

Cam's shoulders slumped, but he didn't seem entirely deterred.

"Hey, your food is ready," the cashier called out to them.

Amber mustered her best scolding glare for Cam, then began to walk over to the counter, the aroma of pizza and pretzels wafting to her nostrils. She opened her purse and pulled out her wallet, fishing through the bills until she found a twenty. She handed it to the cashier and waited for her change, pulling a pepperoni off the pizza and popping it into her mouth.

She quickly licked her fingers when he came back with the change and hastily tossed the coins into her purse. "Thanks."

Grabbing the tray with both hands, she turned and looked up.

Her brother was nowhere to be found.

Eyes widening in alarm, she held her breath. "Cam?"

The scientist looked at her once, then pointed outside.

Throwing the tray down on the table, Amber broke into a run.

"Cameron!"

Chapter IV

THE TRACKS IN THE SNOW

Amber ran halfway through the next car heading to the front of the train and noticed that the door between the two cars was still ajar.

She jolted forward and practically threw herself through the open door. When she stepped off the train, Cam was standing in the snow, his back to her, unmoving as the snow blew around him.

Amber inhaled sharply, the icy cold air prickling her lungs like a thousand tiny knives.

"Cam!" she screamed.

He turned to her, his chin jutted up in the air, lapping up snowflakes as they landed on his tongue.

"Cam! What the hell?" she cried out. "I couldn't find you!"

She tentatively hopped down and walked to him, grabbing his arm. "I'm serious, Cam! You can't ever do that again."

His playful expression faded. "Sorry. I wasn't trying to scare you. I just wanted to go outside."

"Yeah, but our food is back there. I paid for it and everything," she insisted, jabbing a thumb at the train.

"It'll be there when we get back. Let's go see what's on the tracks."

"Ugh. Cam. Why do you have to be so annoying? Can't you just do what your told?"

He was already running ahead of her, and she threw her arms up in frustration and took off after him.

They sprinted a few car lengths before they paused. The sounds of chainsaws and shouting reached their ears just as they finally arrived at the locomotive. Several yards ahead of the train, a giant pile of snow covered the tracks. There were a handful of men with trucks surrounding it. When the siblings edged closer, they realized it was two fallen trees beneath all the snow. The men were hacking at the trees with chainsaws, chips of wood and clouds of sawdust flying into the air around them.

After watching the spectacle a little longer, Amber's eyes were drawn to something peculiar to their right.

It was almost as if someone had cleared a trail through the forest, branches and small trees and underbrush tossed this way and that. And there were jagged gouges along the bark of the larger trees, four, maybe five of them equally spaced apart.

Like claws.

"Hey, you! Get back on the damned train!" one of the men bellowed at them, jolting her from her thoughts. "Train crew can't even keep their passengers under control, and they expect us to clear this shit in less than an hour!" Amber heard him complain.

Cam grabbed her hand when they shouted at them a second time, one of the workers setting down his chainsaw and starting after them.

The siblings ran back to the first car they could jump aboard, looking over their shoulders as they pushed through the deep snow. Amber helped Cam onto the platform, and he opened the door, surprised to find a group of passengers congregated in front of them.

Once Amber closed the door, she pulled Cam to her protectively, feeling uncomfortable under all the strangers' stares.

"Did they say what was going on?" someone asked them.

"When will they be finished?" another person chimed in.

"This is ridiculous!" a third trilled.

A weathered, old hand reached out to them, and at first, Cam recoiled, until he discovered the hand was dusting snow off of his head and shoulders. He looked up to see an elderly man standing there, tufts of his gray hair protruding from a woolen flat cap.

"Has someone been a naughty boy? You'd better be careful or Krampus will come get you!"

Chapter V

THE TRACKS IN THE SNOW

Horror and morbid curiosity flashed across Cam's features. "Who?"

"You've never heard of the Krampus? He comes the night before Christmas and takes all the children."

Cam's shoulders visibly relaxed. "Oh, so like Santa Claus. I don't believe in Santa. I'm too old for that."

"*No, no*. Most certainly not Santa. Krampus is a magnificent white beast with sharp fangs, a long, pointy tongue, and claws the length of your arms. He comes at night and steals naughty children from their beds while they sleep, drags them to his lair in mountains much like these, and *eats* them."

A loud thud echoed against the metal roof of the train, causing everyone to look up.

Cam's face blanched, and he swallowed hard. "It's Krampus!" he whispered and clutched Amber's waist.

The old man's serious expression softened to a

cheerful smile. "I'm just pulling your leg, young man. There's no such thing as the Krampus. It's simply old German folklore."

Amber bent down and met Cam's eyes. "Yes, there's no such thing as that monster. Just snow falling on top of the train from the trees."

The train began to creep forward, and the passengers cheered in relief.

"Thank God!"

"Finally!"

"Maybe we can still spend what's left of Christmas with our families."

"*Blood! There's blood in the snow!*" a woman shrieked, her shrill voice cutting through the victorious exclamations from the others.

Almost in unison, everyone turned to her and followed the direction of her pointed finger. They crowded around the window, trying to see what had frightened the passenger, attracted to the commotion like passersby to a vehicle collision on a highway.

Instinctively, Amber grabbed Cam away from the window and cradled his head against her.

"I don't see anything."

"There's no blood."

"She's seeing things!"

The sound of glass breaking in the locomotive just in front of them combined with metal screeching and crumpling, followed by screams of shock then agony, silenced the dissension among the passengers.

They recoiled against one another, taking several furtive steps backward.

The old man was the only one who moved forward, and he cautiously reached for the door between the first passenger car and the locomotive.

The door retracted, and once it opened, a macabre crime scene lay before them.

The coppery scent of blood and oozing entrails hung heavily in the air, impossible to ignore.

But even worse, the conductor's dismembered remains were scattered across the walls and destroyed control panels, legs and arms, pieces of skull, and chunks of flesh strewn about haphazardly.

The broken windows and gaping holes in the metal allowed the wind and snow to blow through the locomotive, chilling everyone to their core.

More people timidly joined the old man at the door, and they gasped and screamed in revulsion as they witnessed the violent scene before them.

Amber didn't mean to, but as the passengers swayed

and shuffled around, she caught glimpses of what remained of the conductor, and she released her grip on Cam, inadvertently allowing him to inch forward to the front. He wove through the crowd, each step heightening the look of fear and trepidation in his face until it all came to a crescendo when he noticed a bloody clump of stringy flesh hanging from the ravaged metal.

He reached for his asthma inhaler with one hand and sucked in a shaky breath.

"What the hell?" one man's voice croaked.

"Is it terrorists?" another questioned.

Amber briefly wondered if it was the polar bear she thought she'd seen. But she had never heard of polar bears attacking moving trains or being capable of tearing apart metal.

Whatever it was, she didn't want to be around when it showed up again.

Suddenly, massive claws ripped through the top of the train, scraping a giant gash through the metal.

Some of the passengers hit the ground, including Amber and Cam, ducking to dodge the claws as they swiped past.

One of the ones who remained standing wasn't so lucky. He was staring at the clawed arm disbelievingly as it swung down the aisle through the gouge in the train. By the time he snapped out of his paralysis, the claws had already moved past him, through him.

Amber looked up from where she lay covering Cam's body with her own just in time to see the man's torso splinter into multiple chunks and fall away.

Cam covered his ears, his eyes tightly squeezed shut. Then he felt himself lifting away, Amber grabbing him by his shirt and dragging him back as the train car descended into chaos.

Chapter VI

THE TRACKS IN THE SNOW

Amber was running as quickly as she could, tugging her little brother along with her.

She heard pounding upon metal, like heavy footfall leaping across the top of the train, faster than humanly possible. She heard the pounding stop, then metal tearing apart again, felt that cold burst of wind as though there was no protective shield from the elements above them anymore.

Don't turn around.

Don't look.

By the time she put two cars between them, she had darted past the confused faces of other passengers still in their seats, innocent, blissfully unaware of what had happened a couple cars down.

She should have told them to run, to hide.

She should have warned them that something hideous was coming for them, and that soon, they would be in the same irreparable state as the conductor, torn limb from limb.

But she didn't warn them. There wasn't time.

Amber didn't know what compelled her to keep moving forward, to stay calm—she was only aware of one thing: keeping her brother safe at all costs.

The pounding followed them again, only a little further behind them, and she saw the passengers in the new car look up curiously, until the same claws dug through the metal, and the familiar screams and cries and shouts began once more.

There was no way they could outrun it. They would be dead before they made it to the next car.

A slightly ajar latrine door caught her eye, and she shoved Cam into it before closing the door behind them. She fumbled with the slide lock, sorely disappointed with how flimsy the door seemed as she leaned against it to catch her breath.

It was then that she noticed Cam, how his chest rose and fell rapidly, how he sputtered and coughed, how his face was pale and sweaty, his eyes panicked.

"Cam, where's your inhaler?" she whispered urgently.

"I…" he gasped, checking his pockets. "I… dropped… it."

Amber felt a wash of nausea plummet over her. "You

lost it?"

She immediately wished her parents were there, that someone could tell her what to do, that someone would save them. She fumbled around in her purse for her phone, quickly thumbing in the passcode and impatiently scrolling through her contacts to find her mom's number.

"Call Mom... and Dad..." Cam wheezed.

"What do you think I'm doing?" she snapped, cursing in frustration when the call repeatedly failed.

They had no reception. She would never be able to reach them as long as they were in the mountains.

Her parents would never know what happened to them.

And no one was coming to be their salvation.

Two things crossed her mind. If she couldn't get Cam to stop coughing, their hiding place would be discovered. And if they couldn't get his asthma under control, her brother would die.

Amber pressed her fingers to her forehead, trying to remember. Cam had had asthma his entire life, and this wasn't the first time he'd lost his inhaler.

"Okay. Cam, look at me," she said, remembering what her parents would do. He was staring at the door, tears streaming down his face as he listened to the screaming. "Cam. Look at me," Amber insisted again. "Focus. Look at me."

Finally, his eyes roamed to hers.

"I want you to breathe with me, long, deep breaths. Like this." She inhaled deeply through her nose, then exhaled slowly, taking his hand and putting it on the center of her chest. "Again. With me. Inhale. Exhale," she instructed, her voice soothing and steady.

Cam's wheezing diminished greatly, and he stopped coughing.

"There we go. That's good. You're doing great." She held his shoulders and turned around.

People stampeded past their hiding place, trying to escape the mayhem and whatever it was that was attacking them.

A man jostled the lock on the latrine door, shouting for them to let him in, banging furiously on the door with his fists. She released Cam and held onto the latch with both hands, keeping the door closed as best she could. If the man decided to kick in the door, they would be doomed.

Cameron backed into the rear of the tiny bathroom, wedging himself between the toilet seat and the wall. "It's Krampus, like that man said."

Everything seemed to be mired in time, the madness that had unfurled moments before succumbing to silence.

Krampus was a fairytale, folklore the old man had

recounted just to spook them, Amber told herself.

It's a polar bear. One with rabies. It isn't Krampus. That's impossible.

Amber gradually released her grip on the door handle and looked over her shoulder at Cam.

"We need a plan," she murmured aloud, more to herself than anyone else.

"Could we jump off?" Cam offered, mistakenly thinking she was talking to him.

Amber shook her head. She'd seen how fast they were going, how the train was clambering along the tracks unsteadily now that no one was in the locomotive to control it. "We're moving too fast. We'd die in the fall."

Cam thought for a moment, pushing his glasses up the bridge of his nose. "What if we went to the back of the train?"

Amber raised an eyebrow. "What do you mean?"

"I saw a movie once about how you can drive the train from the front *and* the back. They're the same so the train doesn't have to turn around. If we can make it to the back, we can stop the train, and then we can run for help."

Amber had to admit it wasn't a bad idea.

"That means we'll have to go out there. And we don't know what we'll find," Amber said gravely.

Cam nodded. "I know."

"Are you going to be okay? You can hide here, and I'll go out and try to find your inhaler."

He edged away from the wall, jutting his chin up bravely. "We stay together. I'll be okay."

Amber took his hands in hers. "I won't let anything happen to you. I promise. Do you trust me?"

He nodded, and she pulled him into a tight embrace.

Then she stepped back, her fingers lifting to unlock the door.

Chapter VII

THE TRACKS IN THE SNOW

Amber gently pulled the latch back, wincing at every creak and squeak. Centimeter by centimeter, she opened the door until she could see the seats and aisle closest to the latrine.

She crept out into the open, motioning for Cam to stay put.

The car to her right seemed eerily empty and silent, like a ghost town abandoned after a fabled gold rush.

But when she looked closer, she saw the same havoc she'd witnessed in the locomotive. Mutilated bodies and gnawed-upon limbs were strewn everywhere, across seats and tucked away along the aisle.

She swiveled to her left to the front of the train and froze, her breath caught in her throat.

It was just as the old man had said.

Pressed between the seats, a behemoth creature with white fur was hunched over in the aisle, its massive back facing her. Two long, curled horns protruded from its skull, and jagged, pointed ears peeked out from the blood-stained fur.

It made a wet, slurping noise, intermixed with a crunching sound that caused Amber's stomach to flip.

She didn't have to see what it was eating to know it was one of the passengers.

Cam started to move toward her, and she swiftly stepped between him and the creature, shielding him from seeing the hideous beast.

She crouched down to his level and signaled for him to maintain eye contact with her and not look away. Taking his hands once more, Amber began to walk backward so that Cam would only see her and nothing behind them. She cast periodic glances over her shoulder as she navigated the car, increasing the distance between them and the creature.

Cam would stiffen every time he stepped on something soft and mushy, and Amber knew his instincts were telling him to look down at the carnage, but she wordlessly shook her head and pointed from his eyes to hers, then continued to guide him to the next car, making sure to check that the monster was still busy feasting on what remained of the other passengers.

She had almost made it to end of the car when her boot landed on something tall and thin, followed by a crack as it snapped and fell to the ground.

Amber stared incredulously at her feet, horrified to see a partially consumed ribcage surrounding her boot, the broken rib beside it.

But then she heard something perhaps more terrifying.

Silence.

Nothing.

The disgusting crunching and munching noises she'd heard as they snuck past the many rows of seats had ceased entirely.

Her head shot up in alarm.

The creature was now on its feet facing her, its sheer size unable to be contained in the height of the car, forcing it to hunch over.

Its eyes were blood-red, like a smoldering volcano brimming with flaming, inextinguishable embers. Long fangs the length of fingers lined its open maw, and bits of flesh tangled in them, wobbling there, still dripping wet with blood. Its chest heaved as it watched them, unmoving, completely fixated with the sight of her and her brother.

Cam turned and saw it, too, and he screamed and backed up into her.

"Run!" she cried out, and the two of them broke into a sprint.

She chanced a look behind them and almost stopped

running.

The creature was gone.

Just then, she heard a volley of thuds above their heads, and she pumped her legs faster, dragging her brother along with her.

Amber collided with the door to the next car and tried to jostle it open. She heard voices on the other side, hushed ones, and she knew they had barricaded and fortified the door so that no one else could enter. She briefly recalled the man trying to get into the latrine with them earlier, how she had refused to let him in, how it compared to the irony of the moment now.

In a fit of desperation, Amber flung her fists against the door, screaming, piteously begging them to save them, or at the very least, to take her brother.

The pounding above their heads ended, and Amber wondered when the creature would descend upon them, when they'd suffer the same fate as the conductor and the other passengers in the first two cars… torn raggedly limb by limb before monstrously long fangs sunk in to devour whatever flesh still clung to their bones.

Chapter VIII

THE TRACKS IN THE SNOW

And then Amber heard large items being shuffled around on the other side, voices increasing in volume and urgency, and she enveloped Cam, keeping him close to her body in case the creature decided to attack them.

She wasn't going down without a fight. She would protect Cam until her last breath.

"Look!" Cam shouted. He pointed to the door as it gradually slid open, and Amber shoved him forward, needing him to reach safety first.

"You shouldn't have let them in—it's too great a risk!" a well-dressed middle-aged woman snapped to the group of passengers who had moved the luggage away from the door.

"What did you want me to do? They're just kids. Whatever's out there, I wasn't going to just let them die when it's within our ability to save them," a young woman with long black hair and piercing eyes retorted. She gestured for Cam and Amber to take a seat while she and the others hastily piled up the luggage against the door once more.

"Did you see it, what's out there?" another stranger pressed them.

Amber nodded, holding back the bile rising in her throat.

"Well," the first woman prodded with impatience, "what was it?"

"It's Krampus," Cam responded very matter-of-factly.

Everyone seemed bewildered. When Cam noticed this, he sighed. "German folklore says that he comes out around Christmas to steal bad kids and eat them. Didn't anyone in here pay attention in history class?"

Amber looked down at him. "Cam," she whispered. "You just found out about Krampus less than an hour ago."

He shrugged. "Yeah, but I'm a kid. They had their whole lives to learn about him." He turned back to the skeptical audience. "Anyways, we can't stay here. We need to get off the train."

A man wearing a tight sweater stretched obscenely over his muscles crossed his arms. "If you haven't noticed," he began, gesturing out the window, "we're moving pretty fast. I'm guessing this train is cruisin' without a driver. We can't exactly jump off."

"Actually, the back is the same as the front, and you can drive the train that way," Cam corrected him. "We need to get to the back, and stop it from there."

Several passengers' expressions exhibited equal parts surprise and aversion. "We're not going anywhere. We're safe here."

Amber placed a hand on her brother's shoulder. "It doesn't matter how much stuff you put against that door," she chimed in. "The monster can make it through. I saw it happen."

"We're staying put," the man with the tight sweater emphasized. "There's a reason why they're dead, and we're still—"

Suddenly, jagged claws punctured through the metal ceiling of the train, and they swooped down, grabbing the man, digging deeply into his torso and tugging him up through the gouge above. The man was much too large to fit through the hole; there was only enough room for his head. The passengers listened to him scream as the monster yanked on his body, trying to force it through the opening. His skin curled and ripped along the uneven edges of the metal, and the creature pulled up and down powerfully until with one last wail of agony, there was a sickening, wet pop, and what was left of the man's ravaged body plopped down to the floor, skinned and shredded and ruined beyond recognition.

Broken electrical circuits sparked and sizzled around

the hole, and the lights on the train flickered a few more times before shutting off completely.

The remaining passengers huddled down, ducking beneath seats and staying close to the floor, hoping their hiding places would be obscured in the darkness. A few took their phones out and scrambled to find the flashlight feature.

"Put your phone away! It's shining too bright! That thing will see us!" someone hissed.

"It already knows we're in here; we have to get out!" another protested.

Amber's heart was racing so much she was sure the creature would know their location just from the loud, rapid, unsteady beating of her heart. She pulled her phone away from her chest and tried to dial their parents once more. Maybe this time the call would go through. Maybe this time they'd answer.

Metal screeched, and everyone fell silent. The creature was prying open the hole with its claws, making it large enough so it could fit into the car, able to descend upon them like a hawk capturing its prey.

The car catapulted into bedlam as passengers stampeded past one another, scrambling and shoving, throwing the luggage away from the door in a frantic attempt to flee.

Cam saw the middle-aged woman who did not want to

let them in earlier lying motionless on the floor, her body trampled in the fray. Her eyes were wide open, frozen in shock.

Not wanting his sister to suffer the same fate, he crawled under a seat and pulled Amber with him.

Amber grasped his hand. "We have to lay low for now. It'll be okay." She tried to appear calm in front of her brother, grown-up, in control, so that he wouldn't have another asthma attack, but she knew they were trapped. Stuck in the madness, the disarray, entombed in a train full of people who were soon going to be reduced to nothing more than puddles of flesh, food for the beast.

She turned away from him then so he wouldn't be able to see the tears pooling in her eyes and trickling down her cheeks.

Cam happened to look up in time to see the creature's enormous head appear through the hole, its glowing red eyes staring right at him. Its long tongue extended, seemingly salivating just by looking at him.

Amber was still trying to reach their parents, but when she heard Cam gasp, she froze. She followed his gaze and whirled around, inadvertently bringing the phone up with her, its blinding light illuminating the hideous visage of the monster.

So close to her, just above their heads, she couldn't help but scream. But when the creature bellowed and shrieked, retreating to the darkness outside, it took the whole car by surprise.

"What happened?"

"Where did it go?"

The door that Cam and Amber had entered through was finally cleared, and passengers began fighting their way through it. But then Amber noticed people changing their direction, running to the back of the car following an explosion of metal and blood.

The horned creature stood just outside the now-disfigured door, struggling to wedge its giant shoulders through the opening. One arm swatted at the passengers as they fled, while the other dug claws into the metal, shoving it apart, hooves smashed against the floor of the train to try and gain traction.

Amber grabbed her brother and hurried down the aisle. Three other passengers made it out of the car with them, and they all raced further and further into the depths of the train as the temporarily restrained beast let out a fierce howl.

Amber's heart sank, but something within her continued to propel her forward, if anything, to save her brother.

Chapter IX

THE TRACKS IN THE SNOW

Amber and Cam ran through the cars, followed by the three men. They were so close, only a little more to go. If they could just stop the train, they could make it to the nearest town, to safety.

They reached the rear of the train, encompassing a worn seat in front of an array of panels with colored buttons and levers and switches.

Cam looked up at his sister doubtfully. "Umm... which one makes it stop?"

Amber shrugged, casting a glance behind her. "Just try them all."

The adults who were running behind them finally caught up. "How do you stop a train?" she asked one of the three men.

"Hell if I know." He leaned down to look at the controls and pushed a couple, but nothing happened.

Another man reached for the radio. He pressed the side

button. "Hello? Hello? Can anyone hear me? We need help!"

He released the button and was welcomed by a painfully long burst of static. Then a garbled voice answered, *"Copy that. What is your location?"*

The man looked questioningly at all of them, including Cam, who returned the same unknowing look. "Uh, somewhere in the mountains. I don't know. We left from the Cherryton station en route to Piedmont. Bring help now! We're being attacked by some bear—"

"It's not a bear!" Cam interrupted in frustration.

"a *bear* that got onto the train," the man continued. "It's tearing us apart."

"There aren't any bears in those parts," the voice responded.

"And I ain't never seen a bear like that," another passenger agreed.

"It doesn't matter what the hell it was!" the man shouted. "Just bring help! Now!"

"We can't help you if we don't know where you are," the voice repeated.

Amber snatched the radio from him. "This is pointless. They won't believe us anyways. We need to stop the train." She thumbed the button on the side of the radio. "Which button makes this train stop?" When she got nothing but static on the other end, she tossed the radio down. "Just start pushing buttons. Something has to work."

Everyone began pulling on levers and pressing various controls, and in spite of the cold, sweat dribbled down their faces and pooled at their backs, dampening their clothing.

Cam was studying one red lever that sat lower on the control panel than everything else, almost out of sight. His breathing quickened, and he tried to calm himself so he wouldn't bring on another asthma attack. What if the button made the train explode? He would be the reason why they all died.

But that was stupid. This wasn't a bomb.

This could be the only lever that saved them.

Without saying anything to anyone, he wrapped his hands around it and yanked down.

Immediately, screeching and hissing, like nails on a chalkboard, gears grinding, metal against metal, the train gradually began to slow from its dangerously high speed.

Breathless with anticipation, they all waited until the train came to a complete stop. Without thinking, two of the men bolted out the door and leapt into the snow, shifting about nervously to figure out which direction to go.

The third man grabbed Amber by the arm and tried to

pull her out with them. She hesitated and attempted to wrench herself free.

"What are you waiting for? We've stopped!" the man barked at her with impatience.

She shook her head fervently as she stared at the darkness ahead of them, the only light coming from the moon as it cast its beams across the snow. Everything was so still, so peaceful. She could even hear the gentle sounds of snowflakes as they drifted to the ground, the pine trees straining and creaking under the weight of the snow on their branches. "Something isn't right." She yanked her arm away. "It's too quiet. Something isn't right!"

The man threw his hands up in exasperation. "Suit yourself. I'm outta here!"

Cam and Amber looked out into the forest, holding the edges of the doorway, fearfully watching as the men scampered across the tracks, fading deeper into the night.

And then there was a thud in the snow and something darted by them toward the men.

Cam knew it was the creature, and he started to yell to them, to warn them, but Amber clamped a hand over his mouth.

She remembered how the monster had looked at the two of them, how it seemed fixated on them when it peered down from the hole it had created after dragging a person through it.

The other kills were just a distraction for the beast, an appetizer, an obstacle to getting what it really wanted, a barrier between it and the children.

The old man had been right. This was no polar bear, no rabid wolf.

This was German folklore brought to life.

The mythical devourer of children, Krampus.

Krampus bounded through the air and landed on the first man, massive jaws unhinging as it chomped down on the man's head, easily crushing his skull like an overripe pumpkin, blood, hair, and brains spurting onto the snow below.

His companion stumbled backward, whimpering and pleading. He fell into the snow and continued backpedaling toward the trees, but it was too late. Krampus swooped down onto him and raised its long, thick arms high in the air before sinking its claws into the man's torso. With a low growl, it tore his ribcage in two, sternum destroyed and ribs sharp and broken, pointing wildly in all directions.

The last man, the one who had tried to get Amber out of the car, realized it had been a grave mistake to leave the train and wander into open hunting ground. He had already started running back to the train. Krampus grabbed him mid-step and flung him against a tree more than twenty feet away. There was a sickening sound when he hit the trunk, and then his body collapsed at the base of the pine.

Cam was staring at Krampus, and Krampus was staring back at him, clutching the detached arm of his last victim.

Then the beast tossed the arm aside and stomped toward them, its eyes unblinking as it locked on to its prey.

Chapter X

THE TRACKS IN THE SNOW

Amber stepped in front of her brother, her chest heaving. Cam grasped her arm, his fingers digging into her skin as he watched the creature get closer.

She hastily turned and handed her phone to her brother. "Cam, I want you to run. Run as fast as you can, and get help."

He shook his head. "I don't want to leave you!"

She swallowed hard. "I'll be okay," she lied. Amber knew she would be anything but okay when the creature was done with her. She shoved him out of the car. "Go, Cam! Run!"

Cam was bawling, shaking his head adamantly as he began stepping back. "I love you, Amber."

"I love you, too. Always. Now run!"

Cam wiped his nose and started sprinting away from her, away from the train, looking over his shoulder at his sister, watching as the monster closed the distance between them.

He saw Amber, blonde hair flowing behind her, her stance defiant, her fists balled at her sides as she stood her ground before the creature, determined to protect her brother even if it cost her her life.

The beast lifted its arm and hit Amber hard with the back of its hand, sending her reeling into the side of the train. To Cam's horror, she didn't get back up.

It marched toward her with purposeful strides, ready to finish her.

Cam's breathing quickened painfully, and he felt the all-too-familiar feeling of an approaching asthma attack.

He looked at the phone in his hand, and then it dawned on him. His eyes grew wide as he remembered how the monster had recoiled and fled when Amber had inadvertently shone the phone light in its face.

Light! It was scared of light. As the old man had said, that was why it came at night to steal the children.

Cam already knew before he made it into the forest that he would never be able to leave Amber behind.

And even if he survived because of her sacrifice, Cam didn't want to live in a world without his sister.

He activated the flashlight feature on Amber's phone and turned around, fiercely tearing through the branches and snow, back to his best friend.

When he got closer, he saw the beast lifting Amber's motionless body into the air, opening its maw to devour her.

Cam took a deep breath, feeling a sense of calm wash over him.

He screamed as loudly as he could as he drew close to the creature, and just when it whirled around to face him, fangs wide as they prepared to consume Amber, Cam reared his arm back and thrust his hand into its mouth, forcing the lit phone past its gullet.

The monster tossed Amber to the side and spun around wildly, roaring and clawing at its own body, trying to rip out the phone it had just swallowed.

The bright beam of light shone through its pale fur as it slid deeper and deeper into the beast's core.

Then, what began as a small flame following the trail of the phone, suddenly erupted into giant flames as the fire expanded through its thick fur, instantly engulfing the creature, climbing its flesh like a dried Christmas tree.

Cam crouched by his sister's side, cradling her in his lap in the snow, as he watched Krampus writhe in agony, limbs ablaze, until its charred corpse finally sank to the forest floor.

"We made it, Amber," he whispered. "We made it."

Epilogue

THE TRACKS IN THE SNOW

Curled up on the microfiber sofa in the basement, crackling flames dancing in the fireplace, Amber scrolled through her social media for the first time that weekend. One photo she'd posted had garnered a multitude of likes, but that wasn't why she loved it, why she'd made it her profile picture.

It was a selfie of Amber, with her brother photobombing her from the side, less than an hour before pandemonium had overtaken the train.

The photo meant a lot to her. It reminded her of how brave they both had been in the face of an impossible evil, how much she loved her little brother, how she would do anything for him. And after saving her life that night, she knew he would do the same for her.

"Hey," Cam said as he peeked over Amber's shoulder. "You kept it." His voice sounded pleasantly surprised.

She ruffled his hair. "Of course, you goofball." She smiled and set her phone down. "That picture's my favorite." Opening the door to a storage closet in the basement, Amber reached for something, blowing off dust from its surface.

"Mom and Dad are working late again tonight. So..." Her voice trailed off, and she grinned mischievously. "I'm thinking pizza, Sour Patch Kids, a very competitive game of Jenga, and an all-night movie marathon. I mean, if you're okay with that, of course. If not, it's totally cool."

Cam couldn't help but run up to her and hug her tightly.

As he and Amber lay sprawled on the blanket in front of the fireplace watching their second movie, Cam realized he had gotten his Christmas wish after all.

And no matter how grown-up they became, or how swift the passage of time, the deep undercurrent of love for each other would always be there beneath the surface.

Always.

Chapter 4

Damon sat there quietly, staring at the floor, until finally the silence became so unbearable that Cora had no choice but to clear her throat.

He looked up as though the noise interrupted his contemplation. "Hmmmm."

Cora pressed her lips together in a tight line. "So is that a good 'hmmmm' or a bad 'hmmmm?'"

"Why did you make it about a brother and a sister?"

She tensed up for a second, almost wishing for silence again.

Well, this is awkward.

"I think it's a good story. It has the elements of horror, but the kids in it make it less terrifying."

Actually, that's not it at all.

"I don't like that you killed the creature off. Why did you do it?"

Cora shrugged. "Seemed like the kind of ending

people usually want."

"People?"

"Well," she began carefully, "what *did* you like?"

He cracked his knuckles. "I like that you're good with details. I could picture everything as you told the story."

She breathed a sigh of relief. "I *am* a writer."

Holding up her book, he smiled. "I know."

She tugged a little at her restraints. "So are you going to let me go?"

"And where would you go exactly? What will you say when you reach town?"

"I won't say anything. I'll just keep driving."

He gave her a skeptical glance. "Until where, the Pacific?"

She nodded ardently. "If you want me to. I told you, I never saw you or your sister. Take whatever you want."

He looked over his shoulder. "What about that money you mentioned?" But that wasn't what he really wanted. "And the safe?"

Cora's palms begin to perspire, until drops of sweat started dripping onto the floor below.

Offer him the gold. It'll distract him from the safe.

"It's in gold bars. You can have it. But will you let me

go if I do?"

"What gold?" Marisa asked, interrupting them. She had a bag thrown over a shoulder that looked a little on the thin side. When she moved, Cora could hear metal jostling about inside the duffel. Probably the limited jewelry she had left here, her grandmother's. She'd always assumed it would be safer in the cabin than in her home in Virginia. And while Cora never really wore jewelry, she was still upset that this thief would be taking the only tangible remnants of her grandmother she had left. "Because from what I've seen, this bitch doesn't have shit for being such a famous writer."

With annoyance, Marisa snatched the laptop from Cora's desk and added it to her meager stash. Cringing, Cora dug her nails into the wood of the chair.

Not my laptop. Not my stories.

"There's plenty. We don't need to touch her. She can live if she keeps her mouth shut," Damon told his sister.

"She's collateral damage," Marisa retorted to Damon before turning to Cora. "You weren't supposed to be *here*. You were supposed to be tucked away in your fancy house in the city with your family," she finished.

Family.

Marisa's words were like a hard slap in the face.

Cora felt Damon's eyes on her, almost sympathetically gauging her reaction.

"I don't have a family," Cora stammered, her cheeks flushing in shame. "I came here to finish my book."

"I. Don't. Care," Marisa spat at her. "Where is the gold, Damon? And why the hell didn't you tell me earlier?"

"She just now told me," he said quietly, setting the book down.

Marisa was visibly enraged. "So what have you been doing this entire time? Chatting? Why don't you just make her a cup of tea while you're at it, Damon?" She growled in frustration, rubbing her temples roughly. "You are so useless! I thought we could do this together, get some money and start fresh. Get out of this hell hole. But instead, you're literally sitting on your ass while I do all the work." She glared at Cora. "And what, do you like her or something?" Her eyes scanned Cora from head to toe with blatant disdain, taking in her greasy, tangled hair, sloppy clothes, and bare feet that hadn't had a pedicure in a *very* long time. "My, your taste has really gone to the shitter, brother dear."

Cora shifted uncomfortably, feeling like an unwelcome witness whenever Marisa went for Damon's jugular with her insults. A part of her felt bad for the man when his sister berated him.

Maybe telling him a story about a loving brother and sister was a bad idea.

Marisa set the bag on the floor. She reached into her

back pocket and pulled out a knife, flipping it open so that Cora could see the jagged blade.

"We don't have time for this shit. Damon is a lot more patient than I am. Nicer, too. He's always been a pussy. So here's how it'll go. You tell me where the gold is, or I'll start taking things off your face." She straddled Cora in the chair and grabbed her chin, forcing it up and squeezing it between her fingers painfully. "Am I making myself clear?"

Cora's eyes went wide as the blade drew closer to her face.

Just tell them. It's not like it's your life savings. It was just a spur-of-the-moment investment, and you have others in stocks and retirement. You want them gone, don't you?

"Where is it?" She held the knife above Cora's ear, pulling it away from her head and resting the blade in the crevice.

Tell them! It's just money!

When the knife dug into her ear, Cora yelped and jolted in the chair. She could feel warm liquid running down the side of her face.

Her inner monologue went quiet.

"Marisa, cut that shit out," Damon demanded, standing to his feet and grabbing his sister's wrist. "The deal was to rob her, not torture her."

"Screw you, Damon," Marisa hissed, and she got off Cora's lap, spinning around to slap Damon across the face. "Don't touch me again."

Damon gritted his teeth so tightly Cora was almost certain she could hear the sound of the enamel grinding together from where she sat.

"Okay! Okay," Cora acquiesced. She exhaled loudly, trying to calm herself and slow her racing heart. "It's…" She closed her eyes defeatedly. "It's in a hidden compartment in the bedroom, under the floorboards." Cora had made the space herself a long time ago when she first bought the cabin, thinking the small precautionary measure was more reasonable than purchasing an alarm system for a remote house no one would ever try to burglarize.

She never thought such a crime would happen to her of course, but here she was, tied to a chair while a deranged woman attempted to saw off her ears.

"Where in the bedroom?" Marisa pressed with impatience. "I'm not going to dig up the entire floor."

"In the closet," Cora answered unwillingly.

Marisa folded her knife and turned to her brother. "You coming?"

Damon pushed the book under one of the couch pillows. "Someone has to watch her."

She threw her hands in the air. "Fine, I'll do it myself.

Thanks for nothing, bro."

Cora watched Marisa disappear into the bedroom, then looked back at Damon.

He shouldn't want to simply get out of town. He should want to get as far away as he could from his psycho sister.

Damon seemed different than Marisa. Trapped. Eager for something better, but too afraid to leave what was familiar to get it. And certainly too good to be in the company of someone like Marisa, who would only bring him down.

Pretty much the opposite of Amber and Cam then. Strike one, Cora. Well done.

"I thought you were going to let me go. Your crazy sister almost cut off my ear," Cora said, trying to hide her anger. "And you guys were casing me."

He ran his hands over his face. "Like she said, you weren't supposed to be here. I'm sorry. I don't agree with her methods."

Cora wanted to believe him. But could she? "So how did you know this cabin was up here?"

"It's a small town. People talk. You're pretty much the only one in this area who isn't poor so word gets around."

Cora chastised herself for living near such a place, but she couldn't have known. It wasn't like she moved there to make friends. No one except her agent had even been to the cabin.

She'd made the purchase years ago after completing a book signing and speaking engagement in a city a couple hours away. Cora had left the event feeling drained and overstimulated, so she took her rental car and drove aimlessly, rolling the windows down to get fresh air and relishing her newfound alone time. The further she drove deeper into the mountains, the more she fell in love with the panoramic views and the uninterrupted peace and tranquility. She visited a realtor on a second trip back and purchased the cabin on the same day she viewed the property.

Cora chided herself even more for ever telling anyone in the town that she was a writer. She didn't have any friends there, but all it took was a simple mention, a conversation in passing with a friendly cashier in the checkout line at the grocery store, a gas station attendant… Word spread fast, especially in a town where everyone was living at or below the poverty line.

But she couldn't remember a time when she'd told anyone *where* she actually lived.

"If it means anything," he offered, "we were planning to break in, take what we could, and then leave. Hurting you was never part of the plan."

"Well," she said bitterly, tilting her head at the blood making its way down her ear, "it's a little late for that!"

After sitting in silence for a minute, Cora prodded, "Your sister said you were trying to get out?"

"That was the plan. Leave, and don't look back."

"Where would you go?"

He gave her a knowing smile. "You really think I'd tell you that?"

She nodded. "Fair." Then she motioned to the bedroom. "Aren't you curious to see how much all that gold in there is worth? There's cash, too."

"Sure," he replied, but his tone implied otherwise. He had reached for the book again, passing it from one hand to the other thoughtfully.

"It's going to take her a while to loosen up the boards and dig everything out. Every time I need cash, I grab enough to last me because it's such a pain to get it out to begin with. You might want to help her," Cora tried.

"Yeah, not going to happen. And I figure if you could do it, then my sister is more than capable."

"Thanks." She leaned back into the chair. "Well, my closet is a mess. So get comfortable. It'll be a while."

"Good," Damon told her. "Because I want to hear another story." He rested his boots on the coffee table, waiting for her to begin. "And this time, add that creature character back in there."

Cora wanted to protest, to tell him the deal had been

for one story. But she also knew she wasn't in a position to negotiate. She was tied to a chair, no help was on the way, and his sister was ready to chop her up into little pieces.

Damon was her only hope of getting out alive.

THE TOWN IN THE MOUNTAIN

Chapter I

THE TOWN IN THE MOUNTAIN

San Bordelo Mountain Pass

It was their first Christmas away from the kids. Evangeline shook her head and stared out the window at the winter wonderland, the thin glass the only barrier protecting them from the dangerous conditions outside.

They had just begun their ascent into the San Bordelo Mountain Pass. Freshly fallen snow dappled the vast expanse of evergreens, casting everything in a deceptively inviting white halo.

Evangeline pondered for a moment how long it would take to die out there, what freezing to death would feel like. She wondered how much time was needed before her blood would freeze, before her heart stopped beating entirely. Just as quickly, the morbid daydream vanished, and she focused on the tiny snowflakes sparkling along the window, marveling at the uniqueness of each one, desperately trying to think of something to cheer herself up.

It was Christmas Eve. The last thing she wanted to do was think about death.

They would stay on the small two-lane road for almost an hour according to Google Maps, but Evangeline knew the constant swerving along the curved paths would make her car sick in less time than that. She reached into her purse and pulled out a bottle of ibuprofen, shaking out two little pills and downing them with a swig from her water bottle.

Roger cast a sideways glance at her from the driver's seat. "You okay?" he asked.

She nodded silently, turning away from him so that her long blonde hair covered her face, and pretended to be fixated on the passing landscape.

What had she been thinking, agreeing to this?

A mass of emotions flooded her senses... anger, sadness, frustration. There was so much that needed to be said, but neither of them could ever bring themselves to say the words.

Coming out here had been Roger's idea. He was certain a holiday just the two of the them would be exactly what they needed.

Evangeline hadn't been so confident. The thought of not being with her babies on Christmas morning seemed impossible to fathom. Her parents had graciously agreed to babysit the kids for the weekend. But she wouldn't get to watch them open the gifts she had gotten them, wouldn't get to hear their little exclamations of delight as they tore at the colorful wrapping paper and shiny bows.

Christmas just wouldn't be the same without them.

Besides, what did Roger hope to accomplish in one weekend? A miracle where he somehow won back her affections? Inadvertently, she scowled at the thought.

He had rented a cabin in the mountains, nestled in some tiny town that he claimed embodied a Norman Rockwell painting of Christmas. She'd stood beside him as he showed her the pictures from the website. Maybe before, she would have been excited, the thought of spending the holidays snowed in, a crackling fire in a cozy cabin just the two of them, incredibly romantic.

But that was a long time ago, and a lot had changed since then. Sometimes she wasn't sure if she had wasted a decade of her life being married to someone she didn't know anymore.

It was then that he turned on the radio, rotating the dial until his fingers hovered over the knob, uncertain. Mariah Carey's "All I Want for Christmas Is You" streamed cheerfully through the speakers.

Evangeline could feel his eyes on her. It had been one of her favorite songs, and each year, every time it came on when they decorated the tree or drove around to look at the Christmas lights, she would sing it with gusto. Roger used to tell her that she should have been a professional singer.

He reached over and put his hand on hers, and she stiffened for a moment, the gesture surprising her and momentarily sending warmth throughout her body. Then her fingers fell slack against her lap, not affectionately wrapping around his as they used to do when they were younger.

This year, she didn't sing; this year, she was quiet.

Bing Crosby's "I'll Be Home for Christmas" started playing next, and Evangeline sighed, changing the station to another channel. Roger inhaled deeply and moved his hand to the gear shifter instead.

"Are you sure you unloaded all the kids' gifts?" she asked, cutting through the awkward silence.

"Yeah, I got it all."

Evangeline turned in her seat. "Then what are those sitting on the backseat?" she responded accusatorily.

Roger met her gaze. "Those aren't for the kids." He smiled, but it was tinged with sadness. "Those are for you."

Swallowing hard, Evangeline crossed her arms. "I didn't know we were getting each other gifts this year." She fidgeted with a loose thread on her pink sweater. "I didn't get you anything."

He shrugged. "You didn't have to. I wanted to get you

something."

She groaned and threw her hands in the air. "Well, now I feel bad."

Roger smiled again, and this time it reflected genuine happiness. Evangeline couldn't help but remember how she used to feel when he would smile at her like that, when he would look at her like she was the only person in the room, like she was beautiful, important, and special.

"Don't feel bad. Just say thank you."

She shook her head subtly and turned back to the mountains outside.

Wind and snow swirled past them, partially obscuring their vision, and she was grateful that she wasn't driving. Roger was an excellent driver, and even though she was frustrated with him, she knew he could navigate the narrow road. There was no sign of life in these mountains, and Evangeline had yet to see another car since they'd turned off of Highway 147.

Of course she wouldn't. Everyone was home for the holidays, enjoying time with loved ones, basking in the romantic ambiance the season provided. Meanwhile, she was stuck with Roger for the entire weekend, just the two of them, holding a bottle of ibuprofen and nursing car sickness while trying not to think about having to relieve her bladder. It was going to be a phenomenal weekend.

"Roger, I need to pee," she said, pressing her thighs

together. "How much farther?"

"Probably another forty-five minutes. Can you make it?"

Evangeline looked outside. The idea of pulling over and finding some tree to squat behind while she froze was entirely unappealing.

Suddenly she jolted upright in her seat, pointing ahead. "There!" She unbuckled her seat belt and pulled on her down jacket.

A small gas station sat amidst the pines, the red lights of the sign nearly covered with snow.

Roger turned the car into the tiny lot, sidling up to one of the two gas pumps. "I'm going to fill up while we're here."

"Okay," she answered, grabbing her purse and opening the door. Icy wind pierced her skin, and she winced, shrinking into the fur lining of her hood. She ran across the empty parking spots, nearly slipping in her heeled boots, but thanks to her gymnast days in high school, maintaining some semblance of balance on the slick ground.

Shoving the door open, a bell above the entryway announced her presence. A man wearing a red and black plaid shirt was putting cigarette cartons away, and he turned to her when she came in.

"Merry Christmas," he greeted her.

Evangeline blushed. He was tall and ruggedly attractive, dark brown hair and thick stubble spread along his jawline.

"Merry Christmas." She looked around, pushing her hood down. Snow fell to the floor as she did so, and she looked at him apologetically. "Where's the restroom, please?" she inquired, trying to appear somewhat composed even though she was about to lose control of her bladder.

He pointed behind her, and she thanked him and dashed off, quickly opening and closing the door to the single stall.

When she was done, she walked to the sink and washed her hands. As she dried them with a paper towel, she caught sight of her reflection. Her cheeks were rosy, her hair tousled about her face messily, sexily. But she had forgotten how to feel sexy, how to feel loved. Her green eyes held a sadness in them that didn't seem to go away. She was always smiling when around her family and her friends, especially the children. That was what they needed, and so that was what she did. Only in complete solitude, with no one else around, did her face match the devastation in her heart. Then she would cry, she would scream, she would battle the torment that had been plaguing her for so many months. Evangeline just wanted to be happy again.

Her thoughts drifted to the man in the store. It was hard not to; he was handsome in a way that was difficult to ignore.

What if...?

Her heart started thumping harder, faster. This wasn't the life she had planned for herself, being married to a man who didn't even notice that she was sinking further and further into despair.

What if she ran away with this handsome stranger? What if she left Roger and never looked back? Maybe a fresh start was all she needed to feel whole again. Then she thought of their children. She could never abandon them.

But sometimes she wished she could do something for herself and not worry about the consequences. She knew it was terribly wrong to think like that, and she felt like an awful human being for doing so, but Evangeline had been putting the needs of everyone else ahead of her own for so long that she didn't even remember what made her happy anymore.

She closed her eyes.

It didn't matter that this stranger had noticed her. The one man in the whole world who should have didn't even look up from his phone when she came into the room. He didn't bother kissing her good night before bed. He would rather watch hours and hours of television than ask her about her day. He didn't appreciate everything she did for the family, for him. She couldn't even remember the last time they'd made love. Did he even want her anymore?

Still, in spite of all of this, Roger would always have her heart. It didn't matter how much she resented him, that love didn't fade. And it wasn't just because he was the father of her children. His neglect had caused her a great deal of pain. But Roger held the key to her heart, body, and soul, and no matter how hard it was to stay married to him, to remember why she loved him, the negatives could not overshadow the precious moments they'd created for over a decade.

Guiltily pushing her hair away from her face, she threw the paper towel away and left the bathroom. As she stepped through the aisles, bright orange wrapping caught her eye. Reese's peanut butter cups were Roger's favorite snack.

Evangeline paused for a moment in front of the candy. Roger was trying. He was trying to fix things and somehow win her back. He knew as well as she did that it would probably be impossible, but here he was, planning a romantic weekend in a Christmas town.

Impulsively, she grabbed a couple Reese's and walked to the register.

She hadn't gotten him a Christmas present this year. But maybe, just maybe, she could stop being bitter, and she could start trying, too.

Chapter II

THE TOWN IN THE MOUNTAIN

P^{op!}

The car began to thud rapidly. Turning the wheel to the right, Roger could feel the vehicle starting to veer. Evangeline sat up straight, groggily looking around, her hands clutching the sides of her seat in alarm.

"What happened?" she murmured.

"I... I don't know. The tire..." He struggled to keep the car on the road as it thumped along. "We must have hit something."

Evangeline groaned in dismay, fully awake now. It was becoming harder and harder to see the lines on the road with all of the snow covering the gravel.

Roger pulled the car over as far as he could on the two-lane road and switched on the emergency lights.

"We've got a spare in the back; don't worry, Evie. This should just take a second."

When he got out of the car, Evangeline opened her door and followed him.

She looked around. They were so high in the mountains. Her ears felt heavy and full, almost like she was flying on an airplane and trying to adjust to the altitude. She opened and closed her jaw a few times to pop her ears and relieve the pressure. When that didn't work, she let out an exasperated sigh.

Roger glanced at her as he opened the trunk. "I told you not to worry. I'll take care of it."

Evangeline crossed her arms. "I'm not worrying!" She pulled out her cell phone. "Let's just call roadside." She waved her phone around. "Phenomenal. I don't have any reception." She looked at Roger. "Check yours."

Roger fished his iPhone out of his pocket, then turned it to her to show her the unwelcome wording across the top of the screen: "No Service."

She grabbed it out of his hand and waved both phones around impatiently. "You just weren't holding it high enough."

Roger knew that her stubbornness was a double-edged sword, slicing into his patience while also reminding him why he loved her. His thoughts were interrupted by a barrage of sharp, tiny snowflakes colliding into his eyes. He squinted and rubbed them away with annoyance.

"When is the last time you checked the spare?"

Evangeline asked, this time worry trailing each word noticeably.

As they walked to the back of the car, Roger shrugged, half grinning. "I'm sure it's fine. I mean, it's been a couple years," he added as he fumbled with the car keys to open the trunk, his hands shaking from the cold.

Several bottles of wine, two suitcases, and a laptop bag, all essential items for the upcoming weekend, were packed together snugly, but Roger shifted everything aside to get to the spare tire.

Evangeline heard him mumbling to himself.

Something was wrong. He only did that when he was nervous.

"What is it?"

"Okay, so there is good news and bad—" Roger couldn't finish his sentence before Evangeline pushed through to see for herself.

The spare tire wasn't there.

She stared hard at the empty space where the tire should have been, disbelieving.

"So I think I know what happened," he began. "A while back, I had a flat tire and had to use—"

Evangeline reached around him and grabbed a bottle of wine and moved back toward the passenger side door. She hastily got into the car and slammed the door shut behind her.

Roger stood by the trunk of the car, alone, wishing he'd replaced the spare tire when he had used it last. He didn't want to mess this trip up. While neither of them would acknowledge it, he knew deep down that this was their last stand, their Alamo, one final effort to save their marriage before they called it quits for good.

He dusted the snow off the top of his head, then meandered to the edge of the narrow mountain road. In the distance where the sun was setting, he could make out an ethereal glow.

"That's probably it. Damn, we almost made it," he muttered.

He hurried back to the car, opened the driver side door, and grabbed his beanie. "The town is about a mile down the road. I can see it from here." He tossed the keys to her. "Stay warm; I won't be long."

Evangeline waved the bottle at him and rolled her eyes.

"If I am not back in an hour.... keep waiting," he said with a smile.

Chapter III

THE TOWN IN THE MOUNTAIN

With every step that Roger took, he could feel his socks wringing out the water that had made it past the protective soles of his shoes.

He was clearly unprepared for the amount of snow that had accumulated, but it was just a little water; it wasn't going to kill him.

Roger was trying his hardest to stay positive; he knew that things with Evangeline were not what they used to be. He had to admit it was difficult to be away from their kids this Christmas, but he knew this trip just needed to be about them.

"This is where it all turns around," he kept telling himself as he mushed along.

He'd been walking for a little over twenty minutes when he looked up and saw that he was right on the outskirts of the town.

Instantly, he noticed the twinkling Christmas lights, lights that adorned every house and storefront, radiantly beaming, bathing the snow in a wash of warmth and color.

"Whoa," Roger murmured in awe. He began walking much faster then broke into a jog, excited in spite of their vehicle being stranded and his wife most likely drunk by now while she waited for him.

This town was everything Roger had wanted for a romantic holiday getaway for the two of them. Cherryton looked identical to the photos on the website, something that seldom happened in his traveling experiences.

Anyone who had ever visited their house during the holidays knew that Evangeline loved Christmas. She liked most every holiday, but she really went above and beyond for this one with three full-sized Christmas trees and more lights than the whole neighborhood put up altogether. There were always delicious cookies to enjoy in the cookie jar in the kitchen and the aromas of pine and cinnamon wafting throughout the house.

So when the website advertised that Cherryton was *"THE BEST Christmas town in the entire state,"* there was no question in his mind that he had to take her there.

He marveled at the welcome sign that greeted him once he arrived. *"Welcome to Cherryton, where Christmas is a state of mind!"*

And that it was. Main Street was lined with quaint little stores, most of them white with brown wood paneling, like a Swiss ski town nestled in the Alps. The lamp posts, the awnings, and the windows were lined in all variations of

Christmas lights, some of them the old-fashioned bulb lights like his grandmother had that he fondly remembered from his childhood.

And in the backdrop were more glorious mountains, framing Cherryton in all of its holiday splendor, towering out of the darkness like snow-covered monoliths.

As Roger went on, he noticed that one building in particular, the town hall, was far more decorated than the rest. It stood out like a blinding beacon amidst an ocean of light.

He kept walking, drawn to something faint and familiar. It was music, echoing merrily through the town to the tune of Bing Crosby's "I'll Be Home for Christmas."

Flashing lights above peppermint-colored awnings further down the street caught his attention. "*Ye Olde Christmas Taverne*," the sign said.

Roger thought back to Evangeline sitting in the car with a bottle of wine. Knowing her, she had probably finished it. They would certainly need more for the trip.

He wouldn't exactly call them alcoholics, but they both could throw down with the best of them when it came to adult beverages. And as such, he felt slightly guilty that he was considering the tavern as his first stop. Even though no one loved a good, full-bodied wine more than Evangeline, she would be angry with him for not calling a tow truck first.

Best keep moving, buddy.

Roger pulled out his cell phone. Maybe he would have reception here? He pushed a few buttons, but his reflection on the dark iPhone screen was the only thing that stared back at him.

It wouldn't have mattered if he was right next to a cell phone tower at the top of a mountain; the bitter cold had drained the phone's battery.

A light bulb went off in his head. Surely the owner of the bar would have a phone inside that actually worked. He could kill two birds with one stone, he thought to himself with a satisfied smile on his face.

Roger walked across the street, making sure to look both ways as he always did in the big city, then shook his head when he remembered this place was starkly different from the hustle and bustle to which he was accustomed.

The wind kicked up a bit, sending snow and ice swirling about him, and he broke into a brisk jog all the way to the tavern.

A big wreath adorned with holly and a giant red and green plaid bow hung on the door. A full-sized plastic Santa stood outside the entrance, a rosy smile and permanent wave frozen into its design.

Roger chuckled at Cherryton's eccentrics.

He reached for the handle and pulled. The door didn't budge. He pulled again, the grin on his face scarcely fading. Then he tried the door on the other side, pulling it harder. The glass doors clattered against each other, but still did not give way.

Roger's face fell slightly, and he put his hands against the glass and peered in. All of the lights were on inside, everything festively decorated, clean mugs and glasses stacked and ready for use on the bar.

"Hello?" he called out. He knocked against the glass, loudly, but not forcefully enough to break the door. "Hello!" he repeated, this time the frustration unmistakable in his voice.

Roger stepped back and turned around. He would try a CVS instead, maybe pick up some snacks and beverages to bring back to Evangeline.

He started off in the opposite direction from which he'd come, looking left and right.

The snow was falling very quickly now. The road was covered in it, no tire tracks visible. Someone had to be plowing the streets soon. Roger internally chastised the town for not sending out a snow plow immediately.

And then it hit him all at once, like an anvil falling onto him from the heavens. He felt the hairs on the back of his neck begin to prickle and then stand up.

He had already been in the town for fifteen minutes.

Fifteen damned minutes.

And yet this entire time, he had yet to run into another living, breathing human being.

There wasn't even a single car parked on the sides of the road.

The town was alive in every sense of the word, lit up like Times Square on New Year's Eve, but in reality, it was deader than a New Orleans cemetery.

Roger shuddered, but not from the cold, and in spite of every instinct within him telling him not to go, he gathered himself together and went deeper into Cherryton. He was desperate, needing to see someone. Even a stranger's face would have seemed oddly familiar and comforting.

He just needed to know he wasn't alone.

He had ventured past the last block of the town center, and he spun around, a wild, anxious look in his eyes.

This was crazy. Was he going mad? Was the altitude making him sick?

Cherryton suddenly seemed like the most desolate place in the world, a ghost town long forgotten.

Then he saw it, the brief and sudden flickering of light further ahead, past the dark pines, into the forest.

Roger followed that light, his soggy socks and shoes ill-fitted for the weather, causing him to stumble like a drunkard.

He looked down, ridiculously frustrated with his feet,

and noticed that there were footsteps in the snow in front of him.

Following them with a newfound determination, Roger rushed through the trees, toward the fading light, until he finally came upon a clearing.

Before him was a cabin, small and shabbily constructed.

It seemed isolated and out of place, not warmly decorated like everything else. And it had an unusual door, obscenely large and disproportionate to the rest of the cabin.

He was about to run forward to it, something beckoning him closer, but he halted when he realized he would be beyond the protective covering of the thick pines.

Candlelight emitted from the front windows, illuminating two figures rushing hurriedly about, their footsteps audible even from where he stood.

Roger studied them, his unease growing with each passing second. There was something strange about their appearance, clothed in heavy black robes, their faces shrouded in the darkness of oversized hoods.

He saw one of them lift a knife and then plunge it down into something out of view before holding up a furry, limp object and wringing it back and forth as a dark liquid drizzled down. It almost looked like a little animal, perhaps a squirrel or rabbit, but Roger couldn't be sure.

Moments later, the two strangers exited the cabin, each carrying metal bowls that glinted in the moonlight.

Roger watched in nervous fascination as the two figures pulled ladles out of the bowls, then separated and started walking in opposite directions around the perimeter of the cabin.

His eyes narrowed as they flung the ladles out to the side, chanting and mumbling something as they marched along. It was almost humorous from his vantage point, and he wanted to move out of the shadows and ask them precisely what they were doing.

But again, that still, small voice in his head stopped him, and he didn't know why, but he decided to trust it and remain hidden beneath the pine branches.

After a couple minutes, the two strangers shuffled off into the forest and disappeared.

Roger edged forward to investigate what they'd been doing and found himself on a cramped wrap-around porch. He looked into the window near the front door and waited for the moon to slither out from behind the clouds.

A chair was at the center of the room, and rope lay on the floor beside it. Roger pressed himself closer to the glass to get a better look.

A dark ring had been hastily painted around the chair.

And then there was the furry object now sprawled out on the floor. It was so misshapen that he hardly recognized that it was a rabbit, a very dead one at that. Blood matted its light brown fur, and he felt sad for the animal, wondering why someone would mutilate it.

Roger's stomach flopped, but again, he couldn't figure out why, and that unknown was going to be his undoing if he didn't get some answers soon.

Nothing added up.

He turned around and began to walk off of the porch when he noticed a dark substance splattered against the snow. He stepped over it and backed up until he had a full view of the cabin, observing that whatever was on the snow had encircled it.

His eyes grew wide, and he had to know.

He reached down, his fingers shaking, and touched the dark fluid, watching it ooze between his fingers. Raising his hand toward the moonlight, he gasped.

Crimson.

The picture in his mind was starting to form, the puzzle pieces he had been longing to put together beginning to find their matches, and it was an ugly, nightmarish image.

The hooded figures were preparing for something… something that required a ritual of blood to be scattered about this particular structure in a near-perfect circle.

Something was wrong with this town, so very wrong.

The blood.

The cabin.

The abandoned town.

The flat tire.

The flat tire.

Roger felt his heart stop in his chest.

Eve.

Chapter IV

THE TOWN IN THE MOUNTAIN

Evangeline sipped on the Cabernet Sauvignon, swishing it around in her mouth as she stared out the window of their car.

Roger had been gone for more than an hour, and she was starting to feel the effects of the wine, light and dizzy, warm and pleasant. She let the jagged edge of the foil covering of the mouth of the bottle run against the softness of her lips before tilting the bottle back one last time. Droplets of wine lingered on her bottom lip, and she pursed her lips together, savoring the flavor. Placing the bottle down on the floor near her feet, she looked around, boredom coupling with the buzz from the alcohol.

Evangeline impatiently held up her cell phone again, as though five inches to the left or right would make any difference in the reception.

Roger probably wouldn't answer anyways. Maybe she could talk to their kids.

She dialed her mother's number and listened for the

telltale ring indicating that the call had gone through. When it didn't come, she sighed and leaned back in the seat.

Maybe I should just open one of these while I wait, she thought as she fixated on the gifts in the back.

Deciding to be responsible—as usual—she resisted the urge and tried turning the knob on the radio instead, but the music cut out every few seconds, garbled and choppy.

The snow was coming down so hard. Evangeline couldn't see anything in front of the car. The heater was running at full blast, but it was also draining precious fuel. She took the key out of the ignition, but only a handful of minutes passed before the bitter cold seeped into the vehicle.

She rubbed her hands together, fumbling around in her purse for her mittens.

A thump on the roof made her jump.

She edged her way to the windshield and squinted through the fluffy white coating on the glass. It was impossible to see anything. Roger had probably parked under an evergreen, snow weighing down its boughs until they snapped, sending snow plummeting onto the Honda.

She groaned and turned on the car once more. The last thing they needed on this trip was for a giant branch to break off and damage their vehicle. Roger would be livid if he knew she was planning to drive the car with a flat tire, but surely moving it just a couple feet out from beneath what had to be an evergreen wouldn't hurt it.

Sliding over to the driver's seat, Evangeline shifted the gears. Her booted foot pressed the gas pedal, gently at first, then harder. Her brows furrowed as she heard the tires spinning uselessly.

"You've got to be kidding me," she muttered.

She pushed the pedal hard, but snow splattered against the rear window, and she knew that she was wasting her time.

Evangeline buttoned her jacket, pulling the collar up to her ears, and unlocked the door. She would have to dig the tires out in order for them to get anywhere once Roger returned. Sleeping in the car if they got stuck was simply out of the question.

Carefully stepping out onto the ground, she quickly shut the door and exhaled sharply, the cold easily biting through her warm down jacket. Crouching to inspect the rear tires, her gaze wandered from the heavy snow drifts that surrounded the vehicle.

Something black stretched across the road, bits of it protruding from the blanket of white. She stood and moved toward the unknown object, then used the toe of her boot to dig out the rest.

At first, Evangeline thought it was a snake, and she

jumped back frightfully. When nothing moved, she went to it and prodded it once more, ready to leap away at a moment's notice and hide within the safe confines of their car.

But the "snake" was only a thick strip of leather.

She frowned. There was something else.

She nudged the leather once more and inhaled shakily.

Spikes. Sharp metal spikes.

Perfect for damaging tires. Intentionally.

"Damn it, Roger, where are you?" Evangeline asked aloud, no trace of annoyance left in her tone. Only alarm. Although she had consumed an entire bottle of wine, she was sober now.

Somehow she knew it.

It was like a sixth sense, and her heart started thumping furiously.

Something snapped behind her, and she whirled around, her eyes wide and terrified. In her periphery, there had been the swiftest of glimpses of dark flitting between the trees, standing out so starkly against her snow-covered wonderland.

She knew she wasn't alone. She could feel eyes on her.

Evangeline turned and ran to the car, stumbling unceremoniously as she rushed back.

She jumped into the driver's seat and slammed her hand down on the locks, one by one, front to back, panicked.

After that was done, she frantically began searching for something in the car to use as protection. The best thing she saw was the empty wine bottle, and even with that, she felt foolish and helpless.

Roger had a shoebox full of tools in the trunk that he kept for emergencies. But that meant opening the door, going outside, and undoubtedly coming face to face with whomever was out there hunting her.

Taking a deep breath, Evangeline tried to focus. Roger would be back any second. Should she just wait for him? It wasn't like she was going anywhere with the tires stuck in the snow.

It was getting colder and colder as total darkness began to fall across the landscape. Her jacket was warm, but she was dressed ridiculously. Heeled boots and thin leggings. She wouldn't last long out there if she went for help.

And help? Where would there be any help? She debated turning on the heat for warmth, but she didn't want to waste it when she might need it later after the temperatures would become unbearable.

Evangeline leaned across to the passenger seat and pulled on the lever to the glove box, tossing items aside and ignoring them as they rolled around the floor. There had to be something, anything, that could be used as a weapon.

She leaned over a bit further just as the window beside her spewed forward, tiny jagged bits of glass peppering her hair.

Evangeline turned around in time to see a hooded man reach in, only the bottom part of his face visible, gums and teeth exposed from a gap in his upper lip. He raised his arm and swung it into the open window.

She saw something long and dark flying toward her, a baton maybe, before everything went black.

Chapter V

THE TOWN IN THE MOUNTAIN

Thoughts came rushing through Roger's head.

Who are these people?

What the hell are they doing?

Is Eve okay?

Why did I leave her all alone?!

I am such an idiot.

He gathered himself quickly, focusing on the most important question: *What do I do now?*

The answer was simple; he had to get back to Evangeline and make sure she was alright.

Compounding snow on his shoulders sprinkled to the ground as he stood up straight and backed away from the window. He turned from the cabin and headed back toward the town at a brisk jog.

Cresting the hill, he could see the same lights from the town, only now they emanated a different glow, a haunting one. Given the context of what he had just seen, the eerie illusion of the lights made perfect sense; all of the excitement he'd felt when he first entered the town was now gone. He had long forgotten that his feet were soaked or that his body temperature was dropping. None of that mattered because he had to get back to Evangeline.

He'd taken a different way through Cherryton this time, crossing through what was most likely its residential area. He wanted to go knock on the doors and get help, but something kept his feet firmly planted where he stood.

The houses were dark and barren; no one appeared to be home. He wondered if Cherryton was some sort of staged town, and people didn't actually live here, but then he saw shovels and snow plows and bags of salt in the driveways.

He passed by a tiny grocery store, then a church, an all-white structure with a tall steeple. It was then that he could hear a faint rumble in the distance, a misplaced sound against the almost imperceptible backdrop of snowflakes landing on the ground and the electric hum of thousands of busy Christmas lights.

Roger moved closer toward the heart of the town to investigate the noise and changed his pace to a cautious walk.

The rumbling continued to grow from the same direction, luring Roger in like prey to the light of an Anglerfish.

Roger suddenly saw a giant silhouette slowly moving toward him in the middle of the road, and he quickly darted behind a tree. He peered around the trunk and noticed it was a truck.

A tow truck, he thought to himself. It brought him a small measure of comfort to know that the town wasn't completely abandoned. However, when he considered the last people he'd come across, the hooded figures scattering blood in a ritualistic manner, any comfort he had felt from the truck's impending presence vanished.

The truck seemed to be a newer model and except for the grill and what looked like aftermarket flood lights, was entirely white.

Best camouflage I have seen in a while.

"What the..." he uttered.

He could recognize that blue Honda Accord anywhere, along with the duct-taped front bumper from when Evangeline accidentally hit the mailbox earlier that year, and he had yet to get around to fixing it.

"Eve, you genius! I don't know how you did it, but you got a tow!"

The feeling of comfort at the sight of something familiar came back to Roger. He sighed in relief.

Maybe he had been overreacting about what he had seen. Maybe people weren't in the streets because they were visiting their families outside of Cherryton for the holidays. Maybe the hooded figures encircling the cabin in blood had been partaking in some kind of harmless mountain ritual he knew nothing about as a city slicker.

Roger began to wave his hands in the air. "Hey! I'm here, right here!" he yelled.

But it was to no avail; his shouting didn't garner the attention of the truck in the slightest. No brake lights, no slowing of speed. He buried his frustration. He was far enough away from the truck that he was more than likely visually obstructed by the snow.

The truck took a right-hand turn, away from Roger. Moving at a slow enough speed for him to follow, Roger jogged to catch up with it, figuring that he would be greeted by Evangeline in the passenger seat, and they would wave to one another and laugh about the whole episode later over dinner.

He couldn't wait to see her. He didn't want to be out in the cold anymore. Suddenly more than ever, Roger wanted to be far away from this ice town. He wanted to be toasty warm under the sun, sipping strawberry daiquiris with little umbrellas while the curtains of the cabana behind them fluttered gently in the breeze coming off the ocean.

He was shaken from his reverie when the truck pulled behind what appeared to be the only gas station in town. When he got close enough to make out the details of the structure, he noticed that blinking colorful lights lined the little windows at the front of the gas station, fitting perfectly with the small-town Christmas motif;

Roger found it surprisingly annoying. Moving closer, he saw telltale red brake lights reflecting off of the snow at the rear of the building, presumably some kind of garage.

Relieved, Roger's shoulders relaxed. The tow truck driver could fit them with a new tire, and they'd be on their way in no time.

Disappointed that Evangeline hadn't appeared around the corner yet, he walked toward the garage. But as he continued, he felt the cold seep into his bones once more, and he shivered. He wrapped his arms around himself and shook his head, chastising himself, knowing that as soon as he saw Evangeline, everything would be fine.

Chapter VI

THE TOWN IN THE MOUNTAIN

Evangeline's eyelids opened to slits, but she closed them again almost immediately.

Her head was throbbing, and although it was dark outside, the glare from the small oil lamp in the room was enough to send waves of excruciating pain shooting into her skull.

She instinctively attempted to touch her face and massage the pain away, but her hands wouldn't obey the commands her brain was giving them. She scowled and felt something sticky tighten above her left eyebrow.

She tried again to move her hands, this time opening her eyes in alarm when she felt stiff and scratchy material against her wrists.

What the hell?

Her hands were bound behind her, ropes slithered tightly around the back of a wooden chair. Surrounding her was a dark red circle on the floor.

Evangeline started panting, her chest heaving as she gasped for air.

Something terrible was going to happen. Someone was going to hurt her, torture her, and the quick and merciful end to the pain would never come.

She was going to die here in this horrible old cabin with its faded curtains and dusty floors. Her body would be chopped up, carelessly dismembered, and her remains would be scattered through the mountains.

Maybe someone would find a bone here or there, maybe clumps of old hair, dragged miles away by a hungry animal.

But no one would know it was her.

No one would ever find her, not the police, not Roger, no one. Her children would never know what happened to her, and there would be no closure.

Hell no.

She wasn't going out that way.

No, she was going to fight; she was going to make it out of here. She was going to see her children graduate from college and start families of their own; she was going to grow old with Roger.

Roger.

She hoped he was safe, that he had found help.

She struggled against her restraints, but her mind spun, and she felt weak and disjointed, like her body was separated from her head. Her fingers were numb, and she wiggled them in desperation. Pulling against the ropes, she winced as her raw skin tore layer by delicate layer.

Something outside jarred her from the task at hand.

Evangeline scoured the room for something sharp, but she didn't have much to work with in the sparsely filled cabin.

It was then that a dark shadow crossed behind the faded curtains above the sink. The shadow was so large that it consumed the window, the moonlight completely eclipsed by its presence.

Evangeline wondered if it was just a trick of the mind, or maybe the moon had simply slipped behind the clouds for a moment.

But then she heard the heavy thuds on the porch near the massive front door, and she knew the shadow hadn't been a figment of her imagination.

The front door was not an option, not now, not while whatever unholy inhabitant intent on doing her harm trod along the porch.

But there was another door, one that represented hope and a second chance, and it was only a few feet from where she sat.

Evangeline rose to her feet as much as she could, but

like her wrists, her ankles were securely fastened to the front two legs of the chair. She sank back down angrily and then hopped up again just as quickly. She didn't have much time.

The chair clumsily shifted several inches forward. Each thump that landed on the wood floors sounded so loud, so painfully loud.

Only a couple more feet, and she would be in front of the door handle. She would be outside, free of the dangers that were surely awaiting her within the old wooden prison that held her captive now if she didn't escape.

The shadow passed by the kitchen window again, and Evangeline moved even faster. She collided against the door, her chin scraping past the metal handle as she landed.

The door swung backward then, and Evangeline imagined the smell of pine, the scent of freshly fallen snow.

But there was only the sour stench of rot, of mildew, and then nothingness, a dark abyss rising up to meet her as she plummeted down the stairs of the basement to the concrete floor below.

She was lucky. The chair hit the cement before she did, cushioning her fall in the most excruciating way possible. Her head smacked the ground, but not as hard had she landed head first instead. Had that been the case, her skull would have burst open like an overripe pumpkin, her brain splattering onto the floor, ropey cords of gray matter sliding across the unforgiving cement.

But the chair had suffered the brunt of the impact, its structure fragmented and damaged.

Evangeline shifted her weight so that she could feel the yielding bits of wood. She slid her bleeding hands down... down... down until finally the splintered ends of the back of the chair greeted her broken fingers.

She had just finished freeing herself from the ropes when she heard stomping above her head. It was odd and displaced, not like a man's footsteps that she had imagined. It sounded like...

Hooves?

Like two heavy hooves.

Evangeline didn't think twice. She scrambled toward a small window above a metal shelving unit and climbed until she reached the top. Her fingertips wedged under the old wood window, she pushed it upward until a blast of cold air swept over her face.

She squirmed her body through the narrow window, her hip bones grinding against the space between captivity and freedom, not caring when skin sloughed off in her efforts or her broken ribs protested at the pressure.

An enraged roar bellowed from inside the house.

Evangeline stopped writhing, her hands flying up to

her ears to shield them from the thunderous noise.

It was not human.

It was not of this world.

She didn't have time to process what she had just heard, knowing only that whatever it was wanted to kill her, and that this was her one and only shot at survival.

She flailed to free herself, even if it meant she needed to cut something off to fit through that space.

She didn't stop fighting until she could feel the softness of the earth beneath her feet. Then she ran and ran, not knowing where she was going, just knowing she had to run.

The unearthly howl followed her, cutting through the quiet of the night ominously, hungrily… a dark, primal calling.

Evangeline ran as fast as she could in her suede heeled boots, struggling through the snow.

A door slammed behind her.

She tried to fight the urge to turn around, knowing it was a terrible idea that would only slow her down.

But she couldn't resist. She *had* to know.

At the entrance of the cabin, she could make out the silhouette of a creature standing upright on massive legs that tapered down into hooves.

It was impossibly tall, arms too long for its body, with two giant horns spreading out from its skull.

Evangeline had no other desire than to put as much distance as possible between herself and the creature. She climbed higher and higher into the mountains. Sweat broke out along her neck and back. Fat snowflakes smacked her face and melted against her warm skin.

Shoving aside low-hanging branches, she continued climbing until her muscles felt like they'd explode.

Evangeline staggered ahead a few more steps then collapsed in the snow, completely spent, her breath coming in raggedly. She tried to calm herself, to steady her breathing.

Her ears strained for even the slightest tremor in the snow, the subtlest movement of branches. But there was nothing.

Crawling forward on her hands and knees, using every last bit of energy she could muster, Evangeline finally looked up.

Before her was an opening, a large, cavernous hole in the side of the mountain.

No trees grew here, no foliage of any kind.

She reached out to it, hesitant yet hopeful, thinking it could be a place to hide for the night until morning.

But she sensed something, and it made her shrink back

in horror.

Despicable, violent things had happened here, and suddenly, she felt all of it, all of the pain all of the suffering.

Tears streamed down her face uncontrollably, and she slunk away, back toward the forest, preferring to face whatever evil lurked out there than to hide in a place where the trapped souls of so many would stay unburied, tormented in unrest forever.

Chapter VII

THE TOWN IN THE MOUNTAIN

The location of the gas station was on the outskirts of Cherryton, set to the east side of the entrance, which was why Roger didn't notice it on his first time through.

Steadily he trudged through the snow, rounding the back side of the gas station. The Honda came into view, and he had never been so happy to see it. The poor car looked so helpless though.

"I'll get you fixed up fast, old girl," he said quietly. He cupped his hands and blew warm air into them to regain some feeling.

Eventually he made it to the entrance of the garage, two cars wide and deep enough for the tow truck. There was a single overhanging light bulb, dimly revealing different parts of the garage as it swung back and forth.

Roger could see a lone silhouetted figure moving about so he quickly went inside the garage.

"Eve!" Roger called out in a cracked voice. He was cold and tired, but he was thoroughly looking forward to seeing his wife.

It was dark in the room, but his vision quickly adjusted, compensating for the brightness emitting from the Christmas lights outside to which he had become accustomed.

Roger immediately stopped in his tracks when he realized that this individual was not Evangeline. Chills running down his spine, he saw that he was standing no more than fifteen feet away from a stranger wearing a hooded robe similar to the ones he had seen before.

"Wha-what? Where is... where is Eve?" he stuttered while backing up.

The words barely escaped his lips before the stranger pounced on him. He was around the same height as Roger, but he felt stronger, and at the very least, he had the element of surprise.

Roger toppled backward hard and fast, thumping the back of his head on the cold concrete. For a second, his vision blurred, but he regained his senses once he felt the man on top of him. The stranger was close, face to face, and even in the hazy lighting, Roger was easily able to make out the man's distinctive facial features that included a cleft palate.

"You aren't supposed to be here!" the stranger spat. "You were supposed to be with the car. With *her*."

Roger's emotions ranged from rage to distress to

misunderstanding; he was hardly able to process the new information.

Struggling underneath the overbearing weight, rolling from side to side, Roger tried to think back to the numerous self-defense classes that he had convinced Evangeline to go to by going himself.

Destabilize, positive contact, position of advantage, he repeated in his mind.

Putting his lessons into action, he thrust his hips outward in a hard, fluid motion, causing the hooded stranger to fall forward with a loud yelp. Roger instantly grabbed his opponent's head, simultaneously wrapping his leg around the stranger's and using his newfound leverage to roll the man over.

Surprised at how well his tactics worked, Roger promised himself he'd write a glowing Yelp review for the course if he ever made it out of this town alive. He'd figured he wouldn't get anything out of the classes that he didn't already know, at least nothing practical. He had never been happier to be proven wrong.

Raising his fist, Roger brought it down with all of his might, cracking it against the newcomer's jaw. Seeing that the man was clearly discombobulated, Roger used what little moments he had to search the counters in the garage for something that he could use as bindings.

His fingers skimmed over an orange extension cord, and he snatched it up and went to work.

Propping the man up against the tire of the tow truck, Roger began to tie him to the bottom half of the tire, looping the cord around the tire base and the axle.

Each action he took felt so far out of character. Evangeline had always said he was too predictable and bland. He didn't even know what move was coming next; it was as though someone else had taken over his body and was controlling him now.

Roger grabbed the jaw of the stranger and rattled it back and forth, something he had seen on TV. The stranger started to open his eyes, and he lapped up the drool that ran through the gap in his upper lip.

"Where is she?" Roger yelled.

"You was supposed to be with her... You was supposed to!" the man screamed back, uttering each word slowly and with difficulty. "It don't matter now. It's too late for her," he muttered, shifting his gaze to the ceiling.

"Answer my question!" Roger punched the side of the truck, next to the man's head. "What's going on here?"

The stranger's wide eyes met Roger's. "It... it comes once at the end of the year to feed. Each year, we get to pick someone." The man grinned, but it was sinister and unfriendly. "We picked you."

Picked you...

The man began to thrash around, fighting his restraints. "I got to go! They waiting for me at the center of town!"

"Who is waiting for you? What comes every year?" Roger's patience was wearing thin. "Damn it, man, where the hell is she?!"

All of a sudden, there was an animalistic roar in the distance, loud enough to place the puzzle pieces floating around in Roger's mind in their correct spaces.

"Oh, no..."

It all made sense. Evangeline was the one who should have been sitting in that chair.

The stranger began to laugh. "I told ya… It's too late."

Roger recognized the direction from where the howl had come.

The cabin.

He stood up from his kneeling position and ran out of the garage into the snowy terrain. The fading laugh of the stranger carried on the wind as the distance between them grew.

In spite of his depleted energy, Roger's pace matched his high school track days.

Eve is in trouble, and she needs me, he thought as he barreled through the snow. He didn't care from what animal that sound had come. It might have been a bear of enormous proportions, but that didn't matter now. Nothing else mattered.

He retraced his steps, easily maneuvering through the sidewalks of the town until he eventually arrived at the hauntingly familiar wooden structure.

Roger would have to be cautious. The hooded figures were a proven threat, coupled with the fact that there was some kind of demon-animal they were feeding also out there.

He stealthily moved toward the same window at the front of the cabin, fervently praying that he would find Evangeline there, but that she would be unharmed.

Nothing.

He pressed both of his hands against the window, confused. Without warning, two arms reached around and grabbed him, one covering his mouth and the other encircling his chest.

It's over.

Chapter VIII

THE TOWN IN THE MOUNTAIN

"Eve," Roger breathed when the hand fell from his mouth. He closed his eyes in relief, knowing it was his wife before he even saw her.

She moved in front of him, holding a finger to her lips.

When he nodded in understanding, she threw her arms around him, her body shaking in silent sobs. He held her tightly, clutching her small frame to his, enveloping her, burying his face in her hair.

"I never thought I'd see you again," she whispered, then pulled away so that she could see him fully. Her stare was fearful and urgent.

Roger saw the dried blood on her forehead and grabbed both of her arms in alarm. "Eve, what the hell happened?"

"Some… someone was watching me," she stammered. "They took me and left me for… for… for *it*." Looking about nervously, she added, "Did you see *it*?"

Roger shook his head.

"It's huge, Roger." She gestured with her hands. "Bigger than anything I've ever seen. I don't know what it was; I could only see its shadow. But it had horns. I don't think it was human." They started walking at a brisk pace.

"I didn't see it, but I heard it. We have to get out of here, Evie. This town… it's bad. The people are up to something." He pointed behind them, back toward Cherryton. "I know where the car is, but we need to leave now." He took a deep breath, trying to steady the shakiness in his voice.

"Nothing makes sense, but at the same time, everything does. The flat tire… I found metal spikes under the snow. It was intentional. I woke up in that cabin, tied to a chair, a circle of blood around me. That thing was outside, trying to get in." Evangeline shut her eyes in disgust. "I think they're feeding it, sacrificing people passing through, people like us."

Roger nodded. "I ran into someone, and he told me things. He said something about it coming to feed every year. I didn't think anything of it until I heard that roar."

They both looked ahead, to the road winding away from them, down the mountain, toward safety, freedom.

Then there was a flash of white darting from one tree trunk to another.

Evangeline's body went rigid. "What was that?"

Roger followed her gaze. "I didn't see anything."

"There," she said, her voice barely a whisper. The color drained from her face, and she clutched Roger's arm, stepping back and pulling him with her.

Roger strained to see what she had, his eyes peering into the darkness. Suddenly, his blood ran cold. Grabbing his wife, he began running toward the town.

They heard branches snapping behind them. The creature snarled and huffed, bellowing as it pursued its prey.

"Don't look back!" Roger shouted as he tugged her along. The cabin wasn't far from the town, only slightly elevated on the mountain and hidden from plain view. As they rushed on, the jolly, inviting Christmas lights of Cherryton shone brightly ahead of them.

Again, Evangeline felt that indescribable urge to look back, to see how much distance was between it and them. Her long blonde hair whipped around her face as she started to turn, but just then, her left boot heel broke. Her hand slipped out of Roger's, and she found herself sprawling across ice and snow.

"Eve!" Roger yelled.

Evangeline began to look up, bits of snow covering her eyelashes, her face awash in red, green, yellow, and blue light.

There were two hooves in front of her.

She was rendered immobile with fear when she saw it.

Taller than any man she had ever seen, it was eight, maybe nine, feet in height. The beast's body was covered in white fur splotched with dark red. Its arms extended to the sides, hideous, clawed fingers the length of her own arms. Two colossal horns were atop its head, twisted backward, and it had a thin, pointed nose, and deep-set, bloodshot eyes that glowed in the darkness.

Its expression narrowed, distorting its features further as it opened its mouth to reveal wickedly long teeth embedded into black gums. Its tongue lolled out and hung there, strands of saliva dribbling onto the snow.

And then she felt Roger grab her and pull her away, just as those sharp, hooked fingers swept forward.

Roger was dragging her backward, but the hooves didn't move, they didn't follow them.

Instead they began to back away.

Evangeline stared, puzzled.

"Roger," she began, her voice raspy. "Roger, it doesn't like the lights!" she cried out as the creature threw its arms up to block its face. It stumbled around, emitting a high-pitched keening.

Roger wasn't responding, just carrying her deeper into the town, determined to get her to safety.

"Roger!" she exclaimed, finally breaking her stare and

pulling out of Roger's grasp. "Look!"

He turned around and saw that the unholy creature was still following them, but at a sluggish pace, clearly affected by the Christmas lights and their incessant twinkling.

He looked at the town hall just in time to see a man rushing up the steps to the large building. Roger was willing to bet that it was the same man driving the tow truck from earlier that night.

Guess my knot-tying skills could use a little work.

"Look! Someone is up ahead! Maybe he can help us!" Evangeline exclaimed.

Roger suddenly remembered what the tow truck driver had said to him: *"They're all waiting for me at the center of town."*

He held Evangeline's shoulders, knowing what had to be done.

"We can't let this happen again," he said softly, but the fear was now gone from his voice, replaced by solemn determination.

She searched his face in confusion. "What do you mean?" Her eyes darted from the town hall back to the monster following them, but its movements were so slow that they no longer needed to run.

"They are going to keep doing this, Evie. It won't stop

with us. It'll happen again next year and the year after that. Every single time this damn thing wakes up and decides it wants to feed. They won't stop sacrificing poor, hapless souls like us to keep it happy."

"What are you saying, Roger?" she asked insistently.

"Look, I need you to get to a safe place. If you take a left up there and keep going, you'll come across a gas station. In the back is a big tow truck. Take it. I just need you to trust me, baby, okay?"

He ran to the side of the road and grabbed a strand of the large bulb lights. Smashing the bulbs against the bannister from where the strand had come, he clutched the shards of the broken bulbs in his hand. "Eve, I want you to run when I tell you to. Will you do that for me?"

She clenched her jaw. "You're coming with me."

"I'll be right behind you, Evie. I just need you to do this one thing for me. Please, baby." "Why can't we go together?" she demanded.

"Please, Evie. We don't have time to argue!" Roger pleaded. "It will follow me; it'll follow the blood."

"Roger!" she yelped in horror as he took a long shard of glass and dragged it across his palm.

Blood streamed down his hand and onto the snow below, a small circle that expanded out steadily.

The creature's head snapped in their direction.

What little time they'd had left before was gone.

"I love you, Evie," he said with a sad smile. "I'm sorry I haven't been a better husband to you. I'm sorry I failed us." Tears trickled down his cheeks. "There isn't anything I wouldn't do for you." He reached forward with his other hand and touched his forehead to hers. "Don't ever forget how much I love you."

Tears filled her eyes as he took a step back. How was it that you realized how much you loved and needed and wanted someone only when you were about to lose it all? How sad was that?

Evangeline shook her head viciously.

Rushing forward, she met him and took his bleeding hand.

She wasn't going to let him do this alone. "Not without you."

"Damn your stubbornness, Evangeline Miller." But Roger's heart leapt knowing his best friend and lifelong partner was by his side.

Both of them stood still in the middle of the road and faced the creature.

The lights no longer seemed to deter it as they had before. It was fixated on the blood dripping from Roger's wounded hand, its tongue lolling about frantically, its eyes wild with feral hunger.

Then it charged them with the ferocity of a bull, snarling and roaring, tearing through the strands of Christmas lights entangled in its horns.

"Run," Roger said.

The two of them took off as fast as they could for the town hall.

When they reached the entrance, they put their blood-covered hands on the doors and shoved them open.

A hundred faces turned to them when they entered, their expressions bewildered.

Roger and Evangeline paused for the briefest of seconds.

Then Roger saw them, hooded figures scattered throughout the room of townspeople.

He grabbed Evangeline's hand and pulled her forward, running past the strangers, ignoring their looks of terror as the monster tore in behind them.

They pushed through the crowd just as the screams started, as the blood sprayed across the white walls and marbled floors.

There were tall windows at the end of the room, and Roger and Evangeline ran right for them, their fingers still intertwined.

They raised their free hands to cover their faces as they jumped through the windows, glass exploding around them just as the room succumbed to pure chaos.

***

Roger and Evangeline rose to their feet, never letting go of each other's hands. As they walked toward the gas station, the first vestiges of sunlight spread across the mountain.

Evangeline hadn't felt this happy in a long time.

She squeezed his hand. "Roger," she said softly, "this was the best Christmas ever."

He raised an eyebrow, but exuded the same happiness she did.

"But I sure am glad we didn't bring the kids!"

Chapter 5

Cora sat there, waiting in breathless anticipation, hoping and praying that this last story would mean her freedom.

It *had* to be.

She wanted to be strong, to be resilient in the face of adversity the same way she wrote her characters, but she was exhausted. The adrenaline from the craziness of the evening was beginning to wear off and leave her feeling depleted physically and creatively.

The only thing fueling her at this point was hope… hope that Damon would keep his word and set her free… and that Marisa wouldn't kill her before he did.

"Well, that was sappy," Damon said finally, still studying the floor as though some grandiose secret was hidden in the wood grain.

Sappy. Great, he hated it.

"But you did have that… Krampus… in there, so I can't knock it too much." Cora breathed a sigh of relief, and Damon smirked. "Do they make it in the end? I thought they were headed for divorce."

Adjusting herself in the chair, Cora replied, "I'd like to think they do. Did it feel like a cliffhanger?"

He looked at her, puzzled.

"I think anyone who went through something like that, almost facing death... I think that would bring them closer together." She smiled. "Well, that's how I like to imagine it anyways."

Damon's cheeks raised, his grin mirroring hers in approval.

It's working. You're getting through to him.

Feeling encouraged to share more, she went on, "The hardest part about what I do is trying to please everyone. Sometimes even the strong fan base isn't enough. I try hard to avoid reading reviews of my books, but a one-star review is like a punch to the gut every time. I want to focus on the good reviews, but honestly, it wrecks me. My friends tell me I'm too much of a realist to be able to hone in on the positives. It's a curse really."

"'*Curse*'... Is that your..." He gestured dramatically in the air. "...your white whale? Getting over one-star reviews?" Damon asked her, shaking his head and not attempting to mask his disdain. "Look at this place. It's not even your main house. It's a 'side' home. And your side home is ten times better than where I grew up." He chuckled bitterly. "You like stories so much, right? Let me tell you one, about a little boy and his mom. Twenty years ago. Trailer park on the outskirts of town. My mom tried the best that she could raising me alone, and we were poor, but at least we were happy." His expression darkened. "Then she met Marisa's dad, and… things were never the same again."

Damon didn't elaborate, but he didn't need to; Cora imagined the memories weren't pleasant ones.

"Meanwhile," he continued, "you probably had parents who threw you tea parties and bought you a pony for your birthday. You got a car when you turned sixteen. And back then, the biggest 'curse' you had was maybe being mad at your parents because they didn't get you the color paint job you wanted on that brand-new coupe." He leafed through her book. "Yeah, that's the type, I can see it now. In *this* town, we don't have that type. We're all struggling to get by. We don't get cars when we turn sixteen; some of us have never even seen a pony. My mom met Marisa's dad because she needed money to feed me. But she stayed with him because in this town, you don't survive trying to make it on your own. It'll chew you up and spit you out." She noticed his lower lip quiver just the slightest bit, and even though he was cutting her down with insults, a small part of her wished he could have had an easier life. "You know what thing I wanted most as a kid? To see my mom happy. To see her have that storybook romance she always dreamed of. But that shit doesn't exist, not for us anyways. You want to talk about cursed? Just take a good, hard look at Marisa and I."

Cora's stomach flopped, and she knew she'd messed up again, dredging up terrible memories by trying to seem relatable.

Before she could respond, the sound of floorboards scraped together, and Marisa shouted, "Well, I'll be dammed—she wasn't lying. Damon, get your ass in here!"

Damon shifted in Marisa's direction and began to stand. He glanced at Cora, but she couldn't tell if he was more disappointed in her for being so petty, or if the weight of the hopeless life he lived had just come crashing down on him.

Great job; the only ally you might have had now thinks you're a stuck-up princess.

"Wait!" Cora pleaded. "Let me go. Once she has what she wants, she'll kill me." She struggled in the chair in frustration. "I told you where to find the gold. There's enough in there to give you both a fresh start. And I told you not one, but *two* stories, just like you asked. I've done everything you wanted and more. Please… please! Cut me loose."

Damon's posture was rigid, conflicted, but he said nothing.

Marisa ran in, her features uncharacteristically jubilant.

"Look!" she exclaimed, holding up a kilo bar of gold triumphantly. "Look! This isn't the only one. There's more, like *lots* more! We'll be set for a very long time, brother." She glanced at Cora. "It looks like you weren't totally worthless after all." Then she sneered. "I was beginning to worry all we'd find in here were your stupid books."

Damon stared at the gold bar, its smooth surface glinting in the light as Marisa rotated it for him to admire. Even Cora couldn't help but be captivated by its sparkle.

She cursed herself for her stupidity, leaving the bars improperly secured under the floorboards. They should have been protected in a bank, in a safe somewhere.

A safe...

Her eyes flickered to Damon. He still hadn't told Marisa, his own sister, about the safe.

Certainly he was interested in it. He'd asked Cora for the code multiple times.

Taking advantage of the lightened mood from Marisa, Cora cleared her throat. "I gave you the gold, just like I promised…"

"And what?" Any joy from Marisa's countenance vanished. "What exactly do you think is going to happen to you now?" she asked with a chilling seriousness.

The color faded from Cora's face as she came to a sharp realization.

They don't need you anymore.

"Damon, please. I know this isn't you."

"You think you *know* him now because you've spent a couple hours with him? You think he's going to save you? Set you free? Damn, you *are* a stupid little twat." Marisa pulled the knife from her pocket, flipping the handle toward Damon. "You created this mess. Clean it up."

Damon stood still for a moment before reaching out and accepting the knife. "You don't know me, Cora. If you weren't tied to a chair, you would never even bat an eyelash at me, or people like me."

No. Don't let her twist this.

"Please, Damon. I gave you the gold! I told you about the safe! I can tell you where it is; I can give you the code," Cora sputtered in desperation.

Marisa looked stunned. "Safe…What is this bitch talking abo—"

Before Marisa could finish her sentence, Damon whirled around and plunged the knife into her belly. He never broke eye contact with her as he violently ripped the blade up to her ribcage.

Marisa's eyes wide with shock, rivulets of blood trailing down her chin, she held onto Damon's shoulders as she slowly sank to the ground.

Chapter 6

Cora screamed, but no sound came out, save for her breath coming in shallow gasps as she tried to process what had just happened.

Marisa lay on the floor, gurgling and choking on her own blood as the life drained from her body. Her eyes were fixated on Cora, her lips moving wordlessly, until they finally stilled forever.

Cora felt a mixture of relief and horror.

She was going to kill you. He killed her to save you.

She wanted to believe it, to trust the voice in her head, but there was something detached in his stance, in his silence.

Shivering, she looked down. There were goosebumps all along her arms.

But so what if he did? Someone willing to murder his sister in cold blood is a monster.

And if he can do it to Marisa, what do you think he'll do to you, a mere stranger?

Cora felt the relief metamorphosize, and in milliseconds, she had never been more frightened in her entire life. She'd mistakenly thought she had somehow won Damon over with her stories, built camaraderie, that he would protect her, defend her, but as she gaped at Marisa's corpse, it was clear the situation was quickly spiraling out of control.

Damon faced away from Cora, but she had an unobstructed view of Marisa's lifeless body, a look of sheer betrayal frozen in her expression.

"Damon, what did you do?" she murmured, unable to conceal her revulsion. "She was your sister!"

"*Half*-sister," he corrected her, but the way he said it, with such callousness, made it seem like he didn't even care. "She was going to stab me in the back."

Cora shook her head disbelievingly. "What are you talking about?"

He wiped the blade on his pants then turned to her. "She didn't know that I knew."

"I don't understand, Damon."

"She didn't know I overheard her talking with her boyfriend about her plans." He hesitated as if he wasn't sure he could share this with Cora, but it also seemed as though he wanted to lift some kind of invisible burden he'd been carrying. "She was going to use me to help her rob you, then once we got back to our shithole trailer, she would leave with him in the middle of the night and take all the money or jewelry or whatever the hell else we found in this cabin."

Cora didn't know how to respond. Yes, Marisa planned to double-cross him, but did that mean he was justified in killing her over it? She could imagine countless other ways to disable Marisa that didn't involve murder.

"My mom married Marisa's dad when I was twelve. She may have been my sister by marriage, but... she's never been a sister to me." His voice caught, but he cleared his throat and stretched. "I have to take a piss. Don't go anywhere," he added with a half-smile.

Oh, good one, Damon. What a dick.

He disappeared into her bedroom, and Cora heard the door shut in the bathroom. She looked at Marisa's body one last time, wishing she could cover her stunned eyes and bloody mouth with a sheet.

But she didn't have the ability or the time. She tugged at her bonds again in agitation, swearing Damon was a fisherman based on the knots. She wouldn't be escaping them anytime soon.

Cora twisted around in her seat, hoping to find something useful.

The only thing even remotely close to her was the bookshelf, laden with rows of books she loved or wrote herself and trinkets she'd collected over the years. The antique ink pen and ink pot caught her eye.

The pen was the only sharp object she had any hope of reaching. With it, she could cut through the ropes around her wrists. It was her only chance.

She jumped in her seat as much as she could manage, trying to push off the ground with her feet and propel herself; the chair jerked back several inches.

Encouraged, Cora's eyes darted back to the bedroom, then she jumped again.

Closer.

Again.

Almost there.

She strained her fingers to reach for the ink pen, her teeth clenched in unshakable determination.

"What are you doing exactly?"

She stiffened.

Damon stood at the entrance to the bedroom, leaning against the doorframe, watching her intently.

He still had the knife in his hand, but the blade had been cleaned.

"What do you want from me, Damon?"

When he started walking toward her, she recoiled.

You're next.

Think, Cora! Think!

"Please. Please. Just give me one more shot. One more story. Just one. I promise you, you'll like this one."

Damon glanced at his sister and sighed heavily. "I guess there's no rush to get rid of the body. It's not like anyone is going to find us out here."

Truth right there.

It was a daunting reality, and Cora tried not to let it shake her as she conjured up another tale.

He waved for her to begin.

"One more shot, Cora."

THE VALLEY OF ASH AND SHADOWS

Prologue

THE VALLEY OF ASH AND SHADOWS

Wichita Springs, San Bordelo Mountain Pass

Gareth Hayes lifted his pickaxe and brought it down hard on the rock face. Wiping the sweat from his forehead, he bent forward to take a closer look at his handiwork. He furrowed his brows, confused. There were only slight chips in the rock. The progress he was hoping to see after cutting away at it for the last hour wasn't there.

The dim yellow bulbs hanging from the walls of the mine flickered momentarily and then went out entirely, catapulting them into complete darkness. The sound of jack hammers and drills came to an abrupt halt.

Generators must be out of gas, Gareth thought.

He stretched his arms out and felt for the wall. A damp chill filled the narrow walkways suddenly, an icy breath against his sweaty skin. This had been happening with greater frequency as of late, inexplicable and random.

He leaned against the wall and sighed, waiting for the

lights to turn on once more. He was getting too old for this.

When the lights came back on again, the frosty air left with it, and the men exhaled with relief.

"Hayes! Did I say you could take a break?" Tony Hibbitt, the foreman, barked at him.

Gareth picked up his pickaxe and turned away so that Hibbitt didn't see him roll his eyes. Hibbitt was a terrible boss and bullied them into working through their short lunch breaks or staying far past their regular hours. If anyone challenged him in the slightest, he would threaten to fire them or would berate them mercilessly in front of the others, like a military drill sergeant yelling at an unkempt private.

As Hibbitt retreated, Gareth reached for his flask on the inside of his coveralls. He took a swig of Jack Daniels, pausing to enjoy his delicious moment of peace.

This wasn't always my life, Gareth reflected. Before this, he was a father to a beautiful, sweet little girl. And he left it all, like a damned coward.

He took another swig, this one longer than the first.

Gareth had been working with this crew for around a decade or so, living in Wichita Springs the whole time. Usually a miner stayed put, unless there were problems with the foreman or work demands fluctuated. Gareth couldn't afford to be kicked off of this gig. The area wasn't ideal, but it was quiet, and he liked that. After leaving

Indiana the way he did, he had a lot of making up to do with his daughter.

He pocketed the flask, hating himself for indulging in his addiction. His thoughts went to his junkie ex-wife, the reason he'd started drinking all those years ago. Gareth swung down the pickaxe in anger.

Still, he was at fault for what had transpired.

A long day at work, too many drinks after, and a backhand to a crying little girl had been the perfect storm for disaster. Before he could register what had happened, the night had taken a downward spiral, and no amount of apologizing could ever fix what he'd done. Gareth had packed his things that night and didn't look back, unwilling to face the consequences of his actions. He spent most of his waking hours at the mine, and when he had a day off, he would drown his sorrows with the only friends he had: Jack, Jim, and Jose.

Years later, his little girl was here, now all grown up, and he finally had the shot at the redemption he'd been hoping for since that fateful night.

It was his first Christmas with her since she was a child, and Gareth wanted it to be special. His daughter needed him, and this time, he was going to be the father she deserved.

Gareth lifted the pickaxe and swung again, newfound resolve burning in his veins. A large chunk of the rock face plummeted down, and he felt a momentary sense of relief.

But when the rock continued to collapse, Gareth

stepped back in alarm.

All at once, the generators shut off again, plunging the men into darkness. A hazy red glow peeked through the crevices of rock.

Gareth's skin prickled. There was no way they'd be seeing a light source this far beneath the surface.

Before he could say anything further, the rock face gave way to a large hole. Gareth took a few tentative steps forward, fear and curiosity pumping adrenaline through his body.

"Hayes! What the hell did you do?" Hibbitt yelled.

Gareth turned to him and shrugged.

Hibbitt glared at him, but his frown disappeared.

Before he could see what had stunned Hibbitt, Gareth felt a sharp sensation in the small of his back, and then nothing at all. His blood splattered across Hibbitt's face as he fell to the ground, slamming his knees on the rocks. Looking back toward the hole he created, Gareth could only see a white blur of who or what had wounded him. He could feel his blood pouring down his abdomen and legs and knew he only had a few moments left before he bled out.

Chilling screams and pleas for mercy echoed all around.

As his life faded from him, all he could think about was one thing.

Olive.

Chapter I

THE VALLEY OF ASH AND SHADOWS

December 24th, Christmas Eve

The bell on the front door jingled cheerfully, causing Mitch Connor to look up from restocking the cigarette cartons.

A pretty blonde walked in, her green eyes wide.

He rested his hands against the counter and gave her a charming grin.

"Merry Christmas."

She blushed and looked about hurriedly. "Merry Christmas. Where's the restroom, please?"

Mitch pointed to the back.

"Thank you!" she said and rushed off.

Mitch shook his head and smiled, rolling up the sleeves of his red and black flannel shirt. What a woman like that, clearly from the city, was doing in these parts was a mystery to him. He glanced out the window, seeing a single car by the gas pumps. A man stood in front of the credit card reader, blowing into his hands before punching his PIN into the machine.

Mitch scratched his head. The gas station sat on a desolate two-lane road that was sprinkled with the occasional pocket of civilization. The couple was clearly out of their element, poorly dressed with light winter jackets not suitable for the freezing temperatures and shoes that didn't stand a chance against the ice and snow.

Presumably, they were headed to Cherryton which was rumored to be a whimsical Christmas town that drew tourists in droves. Mitch had never been to Cherryton and had no intention to set foot in that tourist trap. He'd lived his entire life in Wichita Springs, a mining town comprised mostly of trailer parks in a valley flanked by mountains.

He heard the bathroom door swing shut. The blonde meandered down the aisle and came to a stop in front of the candy before selecting a couple Reese's peanut butter cups.

She looked down shyly as she paid for the chocolate, long, dark lashes skimming her cheeks.

"Thank you," she told him and quickly grabbed the treats. The bell above the door jingled again as she left.

"Merry Christmas," he mumbled, running a hand through his hair. Mitch had almost forgotten that tomorrow was Christmas. It wasn't like he'd put up a tree this year or spent his free time baking Christmas cookies. The holidays were blurred together these days, and he had stopped celebrating them a long time ago.

Mitch watched the blonde walk out to her car. He rapped his knuckles against the counter before brushing his fingertips across his back pocket. He pulled at the corner of something cold and metallic, but slid it back in just as quickly.

He longed for a better life, a life filled with purpose and love and happiness, but Mitch doubted he would see that dream come to fruition as long as he stayed in Wichita Springs.

A few minutes later, an old man slowly sauntered into the store. His eyebrows were bushy and white, and tufts of gray hair popped out around his woolen flat cap. He waved at Mitch, his cheeks rosy as he dusted snow off of his coat. "Merry Christmas, young man!"

Mitch nodded to him. The old man made his way to the coffee pot next to the fountain drink dispenser. When he arrived at the cash register, he saw something that caught his eye and reached down to grab it. "Might as well get this, too!" he added, sliding a Snickers bar along the counter.

"Headed anywhere for the holidays?" Mitch asked him. It was a stupid question feigning familiarity and interest since most everyone who came to the gas station was just passing through. Mitch didn't really care, and he had no plans himself, but he felt like it was the polite question to ask this time of year.

"Going to the Cherryton train station to visit my son and his family for Christmas in Piedmont." He pulled out his wallet. "Twenty on pump two, and whatever all this mess is."

Mitch wavered for the briefest of seconds, then ran up the items while the old man watched the snow fall outside. "It's mighty fine out there, all that snow. Like a snow globe or somethin', don't ya think?"

"Sure," Mitch replied. "That'll be twenty-four dollars and forty cents."

The old man's eyebrows lifted suddenly, his mouth forming a perfect "o" in surprise. "Prices are goin' up, eh?" He grabbed the Snickers and his coffee, then held the candy bar up triumphantly. "My son has been telling me for ten years to stop eating this garbage seein' as I'm a diabetic," he said, leaning in to confide in Mitch. "But what he doesn't know won't hurt him." He grinned jovially and chuckled to himself.

"Hey, you only live once," Mitch responded, mirroring the man's chuckle a bit awkwardly.

The old man paused at the door, his hand hovering over the handle. "Hey, I didn't ask you about your plans for Christmas."

Mitch shrugged. "Nothing special. I'll probably just spend it with my mom in Wichita Springs."

The man nodded. "That sounds special to me. What I wouldn't give to enjoy Christmas with my mother again. Don't ever take your parents for granted, son. They won't be around forever." Tipping his hat at him, he hobbled out the door to a Caprice Classic parked in the front.

Mitch closed the cash register and pulled a lottery ticket from the roll in front of him.

"Thank you, Grandpa Christmas," he said, taking a coin from a plastic bowl of pennies to scratch at the ticket. The old man was the first person who might have noticed the extra dollar tacked onto his bill. Mitch should have known better; older folks were notorious for being penny pinchers.

Mitch had never been caught, but he figured he had nothing to lose even if he did. What was the worst that could happen? He would get fired?

While he'd never had any big plans to be a doctor or a lawyer, he definitely hadn't imagined his future working as a gas station attendant on a desolate mountain pass. Maybe one day he'd hit the jackpot, and when he did, he and his mother would be on the first train out.

***

Mitch wasn't scheduled to get off the clock until later that evening, but he decided to close the store early as the snow was accumulating quickly on the roads, and he had a perilous drive ahead of him to get to Wichita Springs. He grabbed his jacket and threw the unlucky lottery ticket in the trash can to join the other crumpled up tickets in the bin. Slipping on his gloves, he took the keychain from the counter and turned the OPEN sign hanging on the door to CLOSED.

Outside it was windy and bitterly cold. He hastily got into his old Ford pick-up truck and turned the key in the ignition. Christmas music blared from the speakers, and he cursed loudly and instantly shut off the radio. He held his hands against the vents until the icy air blowing through finally changed to heat, then drove the car out of the tiny parking lot and onto the two-lane road toward home.

It was nearly impossible to see anything through the windshield. The snow was heavy and thick, giant snowflakes piling onto the glass faster than he could wipe them off. Mitch found himself going less than thirty miles an hour, which meant getting home would take even longer than he'd first anticipated.

He didn't know why he was in such a hurry to get home; there was nothing exciting waiting for him, no Christmas feast spread out on the dining room table, no presents under a tree.

Sounded like a downright miserable holiday to add to the countless ones he'd been having for years.

But maybe it was something the old man had said.

He was coming down the mountain just as Wichita Springs came into view, tiny trailers dotting the valley. It was then that he noticed it.

It was almost five, and normally the sun would be setting, shades of amber splashed across the sky as it disappeared on the horizon, giving way to darkness.

But there was no sun.

The sky was an angry, fiery, blood red.

The Ford sputtered suddenly, and Mitch felt the wheel tighten as he lost power steering.

"What the hell?"

The truck was old, but she'd never let him down once.

He pulled off to the side of the road, agitated to his core. Who was going to come get him on Christmas Eve? Taking his cell phone from his jacket pocket, he tried to think of someone who could give him a lift. He made it to the bottom of his contacts list before realizing he didn't have reception anyways.

Snowflakes landed on his face, and he removed his gloves to wipe off the flakes. His fingers felt dry when he pulled them away. When he looked down at his hands, his heart stopped for the briefest of moments.

It wasn't snow that was falling anymore.

His fingertips were dark with smeared ashes.

Chapter II

THE VALLEY OF ASH AND SHADOWS

December 23rd, two days before Christmas

"Chelsea Whitman, come on down!" the announcer boomed as the "Price is Right" theme song played from the television speakers.

The image of the ecstatic guest running onto the stage was blurry at best, white static occasionally obscuring her face. The raucous applause from the audience was unbearable.

Luella gave an exasperated sigh and reached for the remote, her arthritic fingers grasping for the device. She was tired of watching television and needed a nap.

Most of the day was spent in the living room which had been transformed into a miniature hospital set-up, with a special incline bed, heart rate and other vital sign monitors… everything to keep her alive a little longer.

Her fingertips brushed along the edge of the remote, but she couldn't quite get a grip on it. The height of the medical bed mixed with her larger than average size was an accident waiting to happen, and before she could stop it, the bed was precariously balanced on two legs and immediately toppled onto her. Her right side crashed into the corner of the coffee table that held the remote, and a burst of pain shot through her entire body.

"Heeelp" she wailed pitifully, coughing and wheezing over the sound of the television program. She tried to lift herself up, but stabbing pain kept her frozen in place.

Finally, Luella gave up and lay motionless, frustrated tears streaming down her weathered cheeks.

A few moments later, she opened her eyes wide, startled by the slam of the trailer door opening.

Her son bounded through the living room in a panic. His eyes frantically scanned the room until they settled on Luella prone across the carpet.

"Mom!" he cried out, running to her side to help her.

"Mitch," she whispered feebly.

He gently leveraged her until she was upright. "I heard you scream," he told her, breathless. "I thought someone had broken in." Still holding her with one arm, he pushed the overturned bed to its rightful position. "Are you hurt?" His hands searched her face, her arms. She flinched when he touched her hip.

"I'll be alright," she managed, shutting her eyes to conceal the pain.

"Mom, we have to get you to a hospital."

Luella patted him on the shoulder weakly. "I just need some of my medicine. Don't you worry about me," she insisted reassuringly.

Tenderly helping her onto the bed, Mitch pulled the blankets around her. "I'll get them; hold on."

He ran to the bathroom and filled a cup with water, then opened the medicine cabinet. He grabbed multiple orange bottles, reading the labels impatiently until he found the right one.

It was empty.

His heart sank. Walking back to his mother, he handed her the cup of water and some expired ibuprofen. "This was all I could find. I'll head over to Doc Burrough's and see if I can get a refill. Mom, what were you thinking?" he scolded. "You aren't supposed to do much moving around, especially when I'm not here."

But he couldn't be mad at her. If he thought his life was rough, hers was much worse. She never left the house, she stayed in bed watching re-runs from dawn until dusk, and her diseased body made every day a living nightmare.

"It's alright. I'll fix this." He took the keys from his

pocket and leaned down to give her a kiss on the cheek. "I love you, Mom."

***

Mitch stepped outside of his mother's mobile home, paused on the first step, and sighed in relief as he tilted his face up toward the clear blue sky. Snowflakes landed softly on his skin, and he closed his eyes. He inhaled deeply, the mountain air refreshing and calming to his unraveled nerves.

After gathering himself, Mitch stepped down and headed to Doc Burrough's trailer.

Wichita Springs was made up of a couple dozen mobile homes surrounding Mindy's General Store and Diner at the center.

The town was set up so that the only roads leading to it came from the north and south forming a circle around Mindy's. Mitch's mother's trailer sat on the northern outskirts. The mine was located on the eastern side of Wichita Springs, separated from the town by a small lake. The Alvarado Mining Company was the only reason Wichita Springs was still on the map and was the primary source of employment to the townsfolk.

Mitch made it to Doc Burrough's trailer, one of the more expensive mobile homes in the town with a fancy sun room in the front where he hung plants of all varieties and kept Christmas lights up year-round.

Business was good for Doc Burrough. Mitch knocked on the door, waited a second, and then let himself in per usual. Doc Burrough was often too busy creating his medicinal concoctions to notice the knocking at the door. Mitch rounded the corner of the spacious living room until he got to the master bedroom at the back of the trailer. The older man had converted the bedroom into his laboratory, providing the townsfolk with everything from painkillers to antibiotics, albeit in an unorthodox, illegal fashion. Medicine didn't make its way into Wichita Springs easily as the town was so far removed, nestled between mountains.

Mitch opened the master bedroom door and peeked inside.

"In or out, keep the door closed! There's a draft coming in!" Doc Burrough shouted.

He had long, thin hair, the remaining strands that clung to his scalp combed back neatly. Atop his wide nose sat a pair of retractable bifocals. He looked up when Mitch neared his table.

"Afternoon, kid. What's going on?" he asked, hunching over multiple vials before filling them with a powdery substance. The lab looked like something out of a drug dealer's house with burners and beakers everywhere and a centrifuge in the back of the room. But the medicine produced was of the same caliber and quality one would get from a legitimate pharmacy for a fraction of the cost. As rough and tough as Doc Burrough pretended to be, two things kept him making medicine for Wichita Springs: his love of chemistry and his genuine desire to help the people of the town.

"Mom needs more of those pain pills you gave her," Mitch said as he removed the orange pill container from his pocket and handed it to Doc Burrough who took it from him and examined it closely.

He read the contents and then looked at Mitch sternly, wagging his finger at him. "You'd better not be taking your mother's medication, son. This is serious stuff."

"Come on, Doc. You know I'm clean," Mitch replied, taking a seat next to him at the table.

Doc Burroughs stopped mixing the liquids and powders for a moment and studied him. "You're a good kid looking out for your mama like this."

Mitch rubbed his eyes tiredly, dark circles rimming them. "Yeah, well… what the hell else would she do? Can't afford to send her to a proper home."

Doc Burrough removed his glasses and set them on the table before taking off his gloves. "You're doing just fine. You need me to pay her a visit, check up on her?"

"Maybe. She took a nasty fall today. I'm worried she broke something. She needs someone with her regularly." He sighed. "I feel like a shitty son. All she does is watch TV while I work. All day, every day. At least if she was at an old folks' home, they'd have activities and stuff for her to do. She wouldn't just be rotting away in her bed." Mitch felt angry that he couldn't give her more and folded his hands tightly together, trying to rein in his emotions.

"We don't have those kind of luxuries here, boy. What we do have is each other. We're all like family." He patted Mitch's leg. "You sacrificed a lot staying here for her. You could have left Wichita Springs and made something of yourself before she fell ill. You're a good son," he reiterated again. He rose to his feet and fiddled around in his cabinets before filling the orange pill container Mitch had given him. "Here you go, kid. Let me know if you want me to check on her. Remember, we're all family here."

Mitch took the pills from him and pulled out his wallet, but Doc Burrough held up his hands. "No charge this time. Consider it a Christmas present."

The younger man grunted. "If I never hear about Christmas again, it'll be too soon."

After thanking him, Mitch went back to Luella's trailer, placed a couple pills beside her on the nightstand, and grabbed his keys. He loved his mother, but sometimes he felt like his devotion to her was a ball and chain on his life.

He hopped into the truck, and as the last beams of sunlight began to fall beneath the horizon, decided to go to Mindy's General Store and Diner to get something for himself.

Chapter III

THE VALLEY OF ASH AND SHADOWS

D^{rip.}

Drip.

His hands desperately gripped at the gaping wound on his throat as he trudged beyond the entrance of the mine. Blood seeped around his fingers, past his fingertips, and onto the snow below.

He took another step forward, feeling the ground sway beneath him, watching as the landscape blurred and then came back into focus.

There were deep gashes on his left leg, just missing the femoral artery. He had managed to tie his belt around his thigh, but he'd been too weak to make an effective tourniquet. As a result, blood trailed down his shredded flesh in thin rivulets and had soaked his shoe so much that each step he took left behind a bloody footprint.

He thought of his children and his wife at home in Wichita Springs. He had to make it back to them.

The man had barely escaped with his life. It was only when he hid under his friend's corpse that he'd managed to hide from *them*.

Neither man nor animal had attacked him. They were not of this world. He had watched from his hiding place as they'd ripped apart the men in the mine, viciously cutting and slicing at them. The demons were evil in its basest form.

The man turned his head suddenly, but the movement was too fast. He cried out as the flesh on his throat tore a little more, but he gritted his teeth and strained to listen.

The rumble was low and deep. It was the engine of a vehicle.

When he saw a truck round the bend of the road up ahead, he raised one hand away from his throat and tried to wave. Blood poured freely from where his fingers had just been, but he had to try to flag down the driver.

"Help," he gurgled, partially choking on his blood.

A male and a female were inside the vehicle. For a moment, it seemed as though the female was looking right at him.

The couple was his only shot at survival. Between the cold and the loss of blood, he would not last much longer.

***

Mitch pulled into Mindy's General Store and Diner, the welcoming Christmas lights in the windows another reminder of the holiday he didn't care to celebrate. It made him think about the time of year when he lost his father.

There were two other cars in the gravel lot. He stepped out, his boots crunching in the snow as he made his way to the entrance and opened the door.

Mindy sat at the register island that separated the general store from the diner. She greeted him with a smile and a wave, which Mitch half-heartedly returned.

Mindy was in her forties, plump with light blonde hair that fell just below her shoulders. She had been running the establishment for nearly two decades, and as it was the only brick and mortar store in Wichita Springs, Mindy was probably the wealthiest person in town. She was also one of the most generous and had on several occasions sent Mitch home with a free to-go box of dinner for his mother.

"Hey, Mitchell! How's it going, sweetie?"

There wasn't much variety in the store, but there was one aisle that always had the answers to all of his problems.

Grunting, he replied, "Just got Mom's medicine." He held up a bottle of Jack Daniels. "Now getting some of my own," he quipped.

Mindy's smile faded. "Now, Mitchell, I only got a

couple rules here. And one of them is that I don't sell alcohol on the Lord's day."

Mitch looked at her in confusion.

"It's Sunday," she explained. "I don't deviate from my rules. You know this."

Mitch put the bottle back on the shelf. With anyone else, he would have protested and maybe thrown an expletive or two into the argument. But Mindy was one of the few people he respected, and even if her faith was a nuisance right now, deep down he admired her for sticking to her principles.

She stood up and went over to the diner side and grabbed a plate from behind the counter. There was an assortment of cakes and pies in a display case. She took a knife and cut a big slice of chocolate cake. Then she reached above the display for a to-go box and included another slice.

"Come here and talk to me for a sec. I've been meaning to bring you and your mom a couple casseroles."

Mitch went to a table in front of a window, but didn't sit down. "Yeah, she's not doing so well. She had a bad fall today. Found her when I got home from work."

She sat the plate in front of him and placed her hand against her heart in genuine concern. "Oh, no, sweetie, I'm sorry to hear that!" Trying to cheer him up, she added, "What did you buy her for Christmas? Please tell me you didn't get her one of those plastic snow globes from the gas station. Those things are just plain tacky."

He shook his head and reached for the slice of cake, taking a hearty bite. "I haven't gotten that far yet. But I have one more day to find her something."

Just then, cold air whooshed into the store as the door was flung open unexpectedly. Mindy and Mitch turned around in unison, and Mitch involuntarily dropped his fork. It clanged noisily against the tile floor, and he scooped it up in embarrassment.

A young woman was there at the entrance, her pale blue eyes anxiously scanning the diner.

"Oh, it's the new girl," Mindy whispered to him, before going over to the stranger. "Olivia, honey, what can I do for you tonight?"

Olivia.

What a beautiful name for a beautiful girl, Mitch thought.

"Ms. Harrison, I told you, you can call me Olive." She hurriedly made her way further into the diner to get an unobstructed view of some of the tables in the corner.

"What are you lookin' for, sweetie?"

Olive pushed back the fur hood of her jacket, revealing long, dark brown hair. "Have you seen my dad recently?"

"Unfortunately, it's been pretty quiet in here the last

couple days. Your dad and the others from the mine are my best customers, but they must be workin' them hard lately because I haven't seen hide nor hair of them," Mindy responded in disappointment. "And to think it's nearly Christmas. That foreman should be ashamed of himself knowing his workers have families waitin' on them to celebrate the holiday. It's downright pitiful. They should be ashamed," she repeated, clucking her tongue in disapproval as she walked behind the counter and into the kitchen to clean off Mitch's plate.

Mitch and Olive stood there awkwardly, and he stared at his feet until finally mustering up the courage to clear his throat and break the silence.

"Hey," he started. "Um… my name's Mitch. Is there anything I can do?"

Olive narrowed her eyes at him then turned away to search the store next to the diner.

Mindy made eye contact with Javier, the lone cook, and shook her head in amusement. "Young love is adorable. Bless them," she murmured, putting her hand over her heart again in true Mindy fashion. Javier smirked and went back to sweeping the kitchen.

"I can… um… I can help," Mitch began again. "I have my truck in the lot. We can cover more ground," he offered.

Olive strode by him, standoffishly ignoring the comments.

"Olive is new in town," Mindy announced. "She just moved to Wichita Springs from Indiana to live with her dad, Gareth. How's about that?"

"Oh, Old Man Hayes?" When he looked at Olive, she was staring at him scathingly. Mitch mentally chastised himself, realizing he'd said the wrong thing.

Olive ran her hands through her hair, stress radiating from her body language, and she ground her jaw and shut her eyes. She pressed her fingers to her temples to try to think of what to do next.

"You okay?" Mitch asked her, concern in his eyes.

"I just need to find my dad," she whispered, but her tone was icy.

Mitch rubbed the back of his neck and looked away. "I know what that feels like. I lost my dad a long time ago."

Olive stopped pacing for a moment. "I'm sorry."

Then just as quickly, she went to the entrance and pushed the door open.

Mindy handed Mitch the to-go box for his mother. "Hon, you should let Mitch help you." When Olive looked at her skeptically, Mindy explained, "He's one of the few gentlemen left—stayed here in Wichita Springs to take care of his mom. You're in good hands with him."

Olive's expression hardened. "I don't need help. I can do it by myself."

Mindy gave her a sympathetic, but disbelieving once-over. "Girl, it is going to be nightfall pretty soon, and those temperatures will drastically drop. You don't have a car; what are you going to do?" She gestured to Mitch. "Don't look a gift horse in the mouth… especially when the gift horse looks like him." Raising an eyebrow and glancing in Mitch's direction, Mindy turned around and headed back to the kitchen.

Once again, they were left alone to suffer in uncomfortable silence.

Mitch put his hands in his pockets, still blushing from Mindy's compliment.

Olive did the same and pretended to be fixated with a water stain on the ceiling.

"I can at least give you a ride home," Mitch proposed at last.

Much to his surprise, Olive nodded in acquiescence.

They walked to his truck, and Mitch opened the door for her.

Once inside, Mitch blasted the heat. "Is that warm enough for you?" he asked after the heat filled the cab.

"Yeah, it's fine," Olive answered quietly. "I'm Olivia. But my friends and family call me Olive. I hate the name Olivia." She sank into her coat, pulling the hood up further than necessary to hide her face.

Shrugging, Mitch replied, "I think Olivia is a nice name. Sounds fancy."

She grunted. "Well, I am definitely *not* that."

Mitch found Olive to have a unique beauty about her, but kept his thoughts to himself.

He drove onto the main road that led south toward the mobile home where Gareth Hayes lived. He knew it well. It wasn't far from Doc Burrough.

Olive stared out the window, silently watching the landscape pass by in a blur.

"How do you like Wichita Springs? I bet it doesn't hold a candle to Indiana."

She pushed her hood back and gaped at him incredulously. "I hated Indiana. I couldn't wait to leave. At least here nobody knows me, and I can start over." She bit her lip realizing she'd revealed too much.

Mitch chuckled. "See, it's different for me. Everybody knows your business, and the best thing Wichita Springs has is Mindy's. I can't wrap my head around the notion that this is as good as it gets."

"Have you never left this place?"

He lowered his head in embarrassment and eventually took a deep breath. "Can't."

Olive stared out the window again. "Your mom?"

He gripped the steering wheel tightly. "Yup."

Suddenly Olive sat straight up. "Did you see that?" She strained to turn in her seat, but her hood was so big and puffy that she couldn't see around it.

"See what?"

Olive cleared some of the fog from the window with her hand. "There was a man in the snow. He was moving so slow, like a zombie or something."

Mitch scrunched his eyebrows together. "No one would be out in this. Too damn cold."

She rolled her eyes in annoyance. "I know what I saw. Turn around."

Without any objection, Mitch slowed the truck to the side of the road and made a U-turn.

Both of them studied their surroundings intently.

"I don't see anything."

Olive sighed in frustration. "I'm telling you. He was there."

After driving back and forth down the road a few times, they gave up and headed south again to Olive's home.

When he pulled in front of the trailer, Olive hopped out and lingered beside the open door of the truck.

"Thanks for the ride."

Mitch gave her a small smile. "Yeah, anytime. I have to work tomorrow at seven in the morning, but if you want, I can swing by here afterwards and help you look for your dad. Or you can meet me at my place. It's the only white trailer with yellow awnings." When he noticed her face fall in dismay, he quickly added, "If he doesn't come back tonight, of course. I'm sure he's fine. They've probably got him doing double shifts at the mine or something. You know they don't get cell service out there."

Olive shifted back and forth on her feet.

"Yeah, okay." She chewed her lip with uncertainty. "You sure you don't mind?"

Mitch remembered what he'd been told earlier that day and realized it was true. "Around here, we're all family. We take care of one another."

Olive nodded appreciatively, then closed the door.

Mitch watched her leave, waiting to be sure she got into the home alright, then finished the drive to his trailer.

Olive finally crawled into bed at two in the morning. She wanted to believe her father was working overtime like Mindy and Mitch had said, but deep down, fear gnawed at her insides. The man she had seen on the road left a heavy pit in her stomach. Had he been a figment of her imagination, a ghost that vanished in a flurry of wind and snow?

Olive couldn't trust herself anymore after the things

she had done to ravage her mind and body. After all, that was why she was in Wichita Springs.

It was just her imagination, her conscience insisted firmly. Her father would be back in the morning.

Chapter IV

THE VALLEY OF ASH AND SHADOWS

December 24th, Christmas Eve

Olive opened her eyes abruptly and sat straight up in bed. The sheets were damp from the sweat on her body. She pulled away the wet hair stuck on her neck and back in disgust before throwing the covers off.

Olive always slept in a sports bra and panties with an oscillating fan on her nightstand, even in the dead of winter. The fan not only kept her cool, but served as white noise, helping her fall asleep when her mind wouldn't shut down at the end of the day.

Some would think that was strange, trying to keep cool in December when most people would be wrapped in flannel pajamas to stay warm. But back in Indiana when she was at Fairbanks, the drug treatment center she was confined to for several weeks, she couldn't sleep without stripping down and turning on the fan. Maybe it was because she had been in withdrawals. It had been several months, but her body still reacted as though she was weaning herself off of the drugs that had almost killed her.

Oddly enough, even though Olive had turned it on before going to bed, the fan was idle on the dresser. She went over to investigate, saw the fan was still plugged in, and pressed the buttons. When the fan didn't start, Olive groaned, thinking it was broken, and that she'd have to buy another one in its stead.

Growing up with a drug addict for a mother, Olive had gotten involved in the wrong things with the wrong people. After a while, her life had become the definition of chaos, and no one could pull her out of the downward spiral. It was a dark period of her life that she would never forget, the reason she was in Wichita Springs with her father. Olive had to flee from what was killing her and pick up the broken pieces and rebuild somewhere.

She peeled off her sports bra and grabbed a t-shirt from the partially unpacked suitcase in the corner of her room. Her father had given her his bedroom and had taken the couch so that she would have a modicum of privacy.

Olive had struggled with feelings of abandonment her whole life after her father left, but in spite of this, she felt guilty for imposing on his life now. He was too old and poor to be worrying about her and her stupid decisions in Indiana.

Once the holidays were over, she was going to get a job and help him out. Maybe Mindy would hire her as a server at the diner.

She stumbled into the living room hoping to see her father sleeping soundly on the couch. Rubbing her eyes, she glanced around, but he wasn't there.

Dad, where are you?

Olive realized it was still dark, but the darkness did not seem normal. Puzzled, she looked at the window, for the first time seeing that the blinds muted an eerie reddish glow.

She edged toward the window slowly, and with one hand, she pushed the blinds aside and peered out.

The sky was pregnant with crimson clouds, completely eclipsing the sun and coating the landscape in darkness.

She stepped back and returned to her bedroom, pausing at her nightstand where her cell phone sat plugged into its charger. According to her phone, it was past noon. She checked the Weather Channel website, trying to find reporting on an eclipse or some other natural phenomenon, but the website refused to load, indicating she had no reception. Olive waved her phone around in the air, even going so far as to stand on her bed in an attempt to get a signal, but she soon realized her attempts were futile.

She yanked on a pair of jeans, a hoodie, and her boots and rushed to the front door.

Olive looked up at the sky. Snowflakes fell around her

eyes, and she wiped them off. When she pulled her hands away, she was alarmed to see that her fingers were black and sooty.

Her first thought was that she had touched something dirty in the house, or that maybe her black eye shadow had broken in her suitcase and gotten all over her clothes. But as she noticed more "snowflakes" land on her hoodie and not melt into the usual droplets of water, Olive swallowed hard.

Like her, others were standing outside their trailers gazing at the sky in confusion. They scratched at their heads and talked animatedly to each other, throwing out possible explanations and hypotheses.

Nothing made sense. Olive was looking up when out of her periphery, she caught sight of something white flashing across the top of one of the trailers.

A scream erupted causing everyone to whirl around.

Several houses down, someone no, *something* was barreling on all fours toward one of the female townsfolk.

Whatever it was moved so quickly that Olive was unable to make out definitive characteristics other than its alabaster skin, and that it was definitely not human.

It reared up on its thin back legs and began to viciously claw at the woman. She shrieked in agony, trying to block its advances with her hands, but her attempts to deflect its blows were useless. Blood spewed across the vinyl siding of the trailer beside her, and she clutched at her abdomen in desperation, weakly collapsing to her knees.

A few men ran to her aid, shoving the creature away from her, but it shifted its focus to them, turning with unfathomable speed and attacking each newcomer until all of them were scattered around it, impotently curled into the fetal position, moaning in protest and pain.

More screams came from the opposite end of the park, and without thinking twice, Olive turned and ran into the confines of her home, slamming and locking the door behind her.

Her hands were trembling, palms sweaty in spite of the cold. She drew in deep, shaky breaths, trying to soothe herself, but her heart was pounding so loudly she thought it would explode.

A high-pitched screech nearly made Olive jump out of her skin, and she pressed her palms against her ears, blocking out the ear-piercing noise.

It sounded close.

Too close.

Olive went over to the large window in the living room, carefully crouching down until she was just beneath it. She painstakingly inched her way up until only her eyes appeared over the window sill.

Mere feet from the steps leading up to her door, Olive saw one of the people who had been attacked earlier sprawled out on the ground. A broken pair of retractable bifocals hung haphazardly across his face.

The man's chest rose and fell, but his breaths were shallow. He was unconscious.

Her eyes widened in horror when a pale, spindly creature crept ever so slowly from underneath her trailer, slithering forward from between the cinder blocks that served as the home's foundation.

It was naked, but had no distinctive male or female genitalia. Its limbs were little more than bones covered with white, translucent flesh and bluish veins. There was no hair on the creature's head, and from its profile, Olive could see it had unnaturally pronounced cheekbones that jutted out sharply, much like a skull devoid of flesh.

It crawled atop the man, sniffing him as it moved along. With a satisfied grunt, it scurried back down to his feet and lifted a hand.

But it was not a normal hand. Instead of fingers, the creature had curved, razor-sharp claws. It spread out the claws and then in one deft motion, sank them into the man's ankles.

His eyes immediately opened, as if shaken from his comatose state, and he howled in pain. The creature struck him once more across the face, and he was silenced. Its claws disappeared in the man's flesh, sunken in so deep they were no longer visible, and it began to drag him away.

Olive gasped and shut her eyes, covering her mouth to muffle the sound.

When she opened them again, the creature was pressed against the window, hollow glowing eyes staring at her. Its claws scraped across the glass, and she screamed, backing away from the window until she was in the kitchen.

In an instant, Olive was running out the back door, not knowing where she was going, but only that she had to escape. Her arms pumped furiously in rhythm with her legs.

Of one thing she was certain… no amount of rehab would ever heal her mind from the images of motionless, bloodied bodies splayed across the ash-covered ground or the wails of despair that trailed behind her.

Chapter V

THE VALLEY OF ASH AND SHADOWS

Olive's legs were burning by the time she reached the white trailer with the yellow awnings. Panic and adrenaline rushing through her, she looked right and then left as she jogged up the steps to the front door. Her hand hovered over the doorknob.

A part of her felt uncertain she was making the right choice, running to safety in Mitch's home when she'd only met him once. Olive had lived in Wichita Springs for a whole whopping week. Was her father alive, or had those things gotten him, too? She had nowhere else to go, no one else to help her, but she felt an odd connection to Mitch.

She gritted her teeth and turned the knob. The door was fortunately unlocked. Where she came from, people had deadbolts on their doors and bars over their windows.

As soon as she was in, she locked the door and leaned against it, breathing heavily. When she turned around, she noticed an older woman staring at her from a hospital bed in the center of the living room. The woman's eyes were wide with panic.

Lifting her hands to show she meant her no harm, Olive slowly approached the bed. "I'm a friend of Mitch's, ma'am."

At the mention of her son's name, the woman visibly relaxed. "Oh, alright then." She didn't seem to be entirely lucid. She looked Olive up and down. "I'm Luella. What's your name?"

"Olivia. But everyone calls me Olive."

"That's an odd name. I think I would have remembered Mitch talking about a friend named after a food."

Pursing her lips together, Olive fidgeted with a loose string on her hoodie. "I guess you can't say we're friends. We just met yesterday. He drove me home from Mindy's."

The older woman studied her a moment longer, then smiled. "Well, regardless, Mitch needs friends."

Olive didn't meet her gaze. She didn't have any friends either, not anymore. If she was truly honest with herself, her friends had been toxic, and in order to get better, she had to let them go. She tried to focus her attention on the danger at hand. "Do you have a cell phone or anything? We need to call the police."

Luella shook her head. "Just the landline." Concern grew in her voice. "I've been hearing screams. What's going on?"

Olive walked to the light blue telephone mounted on the wall in the kitchen. Picking it up, she held it to her ear, waiting for a dial tone. There was none.

"It's chaos out there," she replied, letting go of the receiver. "These… things… are killing everyone."

Struggling to sit up, Luella starting searching for something in the folds of the blanket on her bed. "What things? Wild dogs?"

"I've never seen a dog that looked like that," Olive answered truthfully.

Finally finding what she was looking for, Luella lifted the television remote. "Maybe there's something on the news. I saw the red sky. In all my years, I've never witnessed anything like it. Do you think it's related?"

"It has to be. Everything happened at the same time."

When Luella hit the power button on the remote, nothing happened. She jabbed the button again. "Hmmm. How peculiar."

Olive wasn't surprised. "That seems to be the trend today."

Outside, aside from the red sky and falling ash, all was quiet. From a distance, she could see the bright Christmas lights in the windows of Mindy's diner.

"We need to get to Mitch," Luella insisted.

"Mitch is at the gas station, and the phone doesn't work."

"How did you get here?"

Olive shrugged and pushed her hair behind her ears as she paced back and forth. "I ran. I don't have a car." As if a light bulb went off in her head, she snapped her fingers. "Wait. Do you have another car here?"

Luella looked at her like she'd grown three heads. "I haven't driven a car in at least ten years since I got sick. Anywhere I need to go, Mitch takes me. But I don't get out very often on account of my condition."

Weighing her options, Olive walked to the window once more. She didn't want to go outside again and risk running into one of the creatures. She looked around the room, struggling to see in the dimly-lit space. There were photographs hung on the wall, photographs of a little boy, of a couple smiling on their wedding day, of old black and white portrait shots of a man and a woman with somber expressions on their faces. When she noticed the hunting rifle a little further down, she ran to it and pulled it from its mounting.

"Does this work?" she asked Luella excitedly, turning the weapon over in her hands to inspect it. Olive didn't know much about guns, but she could see it wasn't loaded. "Where's the ammo?"

"No, no," Luella told her. "That's Mitch's dad's hunting rifle. Hasn't been used in over two decades."

"Oh." She returned it to its mount on the wall. Her shoulders were tense, and her jaw was taut. She could hear screaming from far away.

Luella grabbed a glass of water from the table next to her. "My hip is bothering me something fierce again. Can you hand me my pills, Olive? They're in the kitchen."

Olive went to the kitchen and took the pill bottle from a shelf near the sink. There was faded, nearly illegible hand-writing on the label of the bottle, but Olive didn't miss it.

OxyContin.

It used to be one of many narcotics Olive had abused before going to rehab.

She wetted her lips.

Maybe just one.

Just one to take off the edge.

Olive pressed her palm into the cap, ready to open the bottle.

But she didn't. She was drawn to something else.

A photo was on the refrigerator of a little boy wedged between two smiling adults in Times Square. Olive instantly recognized Mitch and Luella. She released the pressure on the lid, and her hand fell to her side.

She took the photograph off the refrigerator and went

back into the room. "I thought Mitch had never left Wichita Springs."

Luella smiled when she saw the photograph. Taking it from her, she pointed to it. "That's Mitch's favorite picture. Took it when we all visited New York for Christmas. Mitch was just seven here."

Olive studied the photo with her. "Is that your husband?"

Luella nodded, and her eyes became moist with the promise of tears.

"What happened to him?" Olive asked. Realizing her impudence, she corrected, "You don't have to tell me if you don't want to."

Luella reached for the pill bottle from Olive, who reluctantly handed it over. "He died of a brain tumor shortly after the trip. That's the last picture we got before he died." She placed a pill in her mouth then took a sip of water. "I think it's why Mitch doesn't like celebrating Christmas anymore."

Olive set the photo down and glanced at the door.

"What is it?"

She tilted her head and strained to listen. "That's just it," Olive murmured. "I don't hear anything."

The screams had vanished, and all that remained was silence.

"Maybe the police took care of it," Olive suggested.

"Honey, we don't have police here. We'd be lucky if a sheriff came out a couple times a year."

Olive quietly went to the window.

There were strange prints in the ash outside. Not human.

The markings seemed to circle around on either side of the trailer.

"Luella, we need to hide," Olive whispered. "Can you walk?"

The older woman shook her head. "Not with you as my support. Mitch always helps me get around. You won't be strong enough." She pointed to the wheels on her bed. "Roll me into his room, and we'll lock the door and hide."

Olive complied and wheeled the bed past the kitchen and through the narrow hallway into the sole bedroom in the trailer. The room was small with a neatly-made twin bed pushed up against the wall.

Luella's hospital bed almost didn't fit, but Olive managed to maneuver it in front of the closet. She had barely locked the door when she heard a crash in the living room.

Wide-eyed, she looked at Luella, raising a finger to her lips.

The cheap wood door wouldn't keep a mosquito out.

She placed her hands on either side of a dresser and scooted it against the door. As soon as she did so, a screech sounded from the living room, and something scrambled across the wood floor until it was just outside the bedroom.

Claws raked the wooden surface of the door, coupled with intermittent pounding. Olive didn't have to see it to know it was the same creature from earlier.

Suddenly the clawing and pounding stopped, and once more, the women were thrust into uncertain silence.

"Maybe it went away," Luella murmured. Her hand was clutching at the neckline of her nightgown, balling the material in her fist, blatantly terrified.

A shadow moved past the bedroom window, and in the next second, a clawed hand broke through the glass, straining and swiping wildly.

Instinctively, Olive climbed over Luella's bed and jumped into the closet. She pushed against the paneled door, trying to slow her gasps of fear.

Luella began to scream and call for help, but Olive rapidly shook her head inside the closet, tears streaming down her face as she sank to her knees, paralyzed in fear.

Through the thin slats in the window, she could see the pale, ghastly creature crawling atop Luella's bed. It inched forward on all fours over her body, hissing and snarling.

The woman begged for mercy, her words choked by sobs. Just as it neared her face, it stared at her for a moment, glowing sockets of emptiness hovering inches above her eyes.

From her hiding place, Olive saw the sharp clawed hands slice into Luella's abdomen, and each time they lifted from her body, arcs of blood would be splashed across the walls.

Olive pressed her hands to her ears to block out Luella's wails of agony. She rocked back and forth in the closet, silent screams forming in her throat, but never leaving her lips.

It seemed as though everything was mired in time, the minutes passing like hours, the hours passing like days.

It had been some time since Luella had been taken away, her body carelessly dragged by the creature across the hospital bed and through the broken window. Olive had heard her flesh ripping as the creature tugged at her motionless form, forcing it over the jagged shards of glass that clung to the window frame.

It wasn't until she recognized a familiar voice yelling through the house that she slipped from her hiding place and waited against the bedroom door.

"Mom!" Mitch shouted. He pounded against the door, and Olive hastily moved the dresser aside.

"Mitch!" she cried, clinging to him as he came in. "I'm so sorry, Mitch."

He looked at her in desperation. "Olive, where is she?

Where's my mother?"

Olive's blue eyes were filled with sorrow.

When he saw the blood and strips of skin along the windowsill, he covered his face with his hands and fell to his knees.

Olive felt a wave of guilt and nausea wash over her. She should have tried to save Luella. Instead she hid in the closet like a coward. She laid a hand on his shoulder. "I'm so sorry."

He stayed crouched for a few minutes, and while Olive couldn't see his face, she knew he was crying.

Finally, he rose to his feet and cleared his throat. "I know where we should go. We can find help there."

Taking her hand, they ran out the front door and down the dirt road that led to Mindy's.

They dodged between the trailers, pressing themselves against the flimsy vinyl siding and paused to be sure they weren't being followed. There was a large expanse of space from their hiding place to the nearest trailer, with no trees or other obstructions to conceal them from view.

"Alright, coast is clear," Mitch told her. "Come on."

They started running again, Mitch faster than Olive. He made it to the next trailer before she did, peering around the corner of it. Only a handful of trailers were left before they got to Mindy's.

They could make it.

"Ready?" he asked. When she didn't respond after a few seconds, he turned around apprehensively. "Olive?"

A horrible screech reverberated nearby.

Those things were coming back, resuming their wicked hunt.

Without even thinking, he burst out from the side of the trailer in search of Olive, not caring if the creatures saw him.

Olive lay on the ground beside the last trailer they'd passed, next to a flowerbed lined with large stones. Some of the stones were scattered, their perfect symmetry disrupted, and Mitch knew she had tripped over them in their mad dash for the adjacent trailer.

She struggled to get up, clearly favoring her left ankle.

He rushed to her side, reaching under her shoulders to pull her to her feet.

Her eyes were wide, and she seemed surprised he was there.

"I think I rolled my ankle," she said, wincing. A thin sheen of sweat shone on her forehead as she examined the injury.

"We'll check it out at Mindy's. For now, we gotta move." Mitch placed her arm over his shoulders, and the two hobbled over to the trailer.

He leaned Olive against the side then checked their surroundings for the creatures.

"Mitch," Olive whispered.

He turned to look at her. Her blue eyes were full of tears.

"I'm so sorry. I should have done more to help your mother." She unsuccessfully tried to hold back a sob. "I hid in the closet like a coward while that thing... tore her apart. I did nothing!" She shook her head incredulously. "You came back for me just now, and I didn't deserve that. You should have left me for them."

Mitch took a deep breath. "This place, these people... they're all I've ever known. With my mom gone, I have another hole in my life. I'm not going to lose you, too."

"But you hardly know me," Olive protested.

"Maybe. But we take care of our own here, and the moment you set foot in Wichita Springs, you became one of us." He blushed a little. "And... you're important to me."

Olive sniffled and wiped her eyes, but a small smile appeared on her lips. "Alright, Casanova." She tentatively put weight on her battered ankle. "I think I can make it."

He wrapped his arm around her waist, and they continued the journey until they saw the bright, cheerful Christmas lights of Mindy's diner, a welcome beacon in an otherwise harrowing storm.

Chapter VI

THE VALLEY OF ASH AND SHADOWS

Mindy's was dark except for a couple strands of Christmas lights lining the windows on the inside. Several frightened people were within, anxiously sitting at tables or standing warily by the windows, improvised weapons and flashlights in their hands.

Mitch and Olive went to Mindy who, true to form, was tending to some of the older survivors with wet rags and bottled water.

"It's good to see you made it, Mindy," Mitch told her, hugging the older woman in relief.

"The Lord's our Shepherd. He'll guide us from this darkness," Mindy asserted.

"How can we help?" Olive asked.

Mindy shot her a smile. "That's sweet of you to offer. We could sure use it. Javier is preparing some food for the others. Would you mind serving it to that table over there?"

Olive nodded politely and went to the kitchen, Mitch not far behind her.

She gave the room a cursory glance, seeing only two men with hunting rifles. "We need more guns. They're going to come here, and we'll have nothing. Throwing pots and pans at them won't work."

"I know," Mitch said quietly as they walked toward the kitchen. Hot plates of hamburgers and mac and cheese were lined along the counter, waiting to be served.

"It's only a matter of time before they find us," Olive emphasized more loudly, no longer hiding her fear. She was frustrated with these people and their lack of preparation. She knew she was being unfair, and that she herself had nothing to contribute when it came to defending anyone, but Olive was battling a mélange of emotions, and her handle on them was quickly dissipating.

Scared faces looked up at them as they went past, taking notice of what she was saying.

Mitch set his plates down and grabbed her shoulders. "I *know*. But we accomplish nothing by scaring everyone in here."

Deep down, Olive knew he was right. Why was she behaving like a pathetic child when he was trying to be brave for everyone else, even after losing his mother less than an hour before? She wasn't sure if there was anyone left on this earth who cared about her, but maybe she deserved that. After all, she'd already gravely let down the one person who was her only friend. Olive inhaled a shaky breath, reached for the remaining plates on the counter, and followed Mitch.

As they both arrived at a table, Mitch recognized Betty and Bill, residents of the southern side of Wichita Springs.

"Well, whatever is happening, it seems like this 'thing' is stopping all engines from working. I tried my truck and my generator, and I got nothing," Bill explained to Betty.

"If that's the case, how does Mindy have these lights?" Olive inquired, pointing to the Christmas lights.

"Mindy is a bit of a prepper. She thinks the end times are coming." Mitch shrugged. "She might not be so wrong after all." The couple at the table nodded in agreement.

Mindy joined them, holding a giant gallon Ziploc bag of various batteries. "I wanted folks to know this was a safe haven for them, so I strung up some of my old lights that ran off AA batteries."

Bill chuckled. "Battery-powered Christmas lights... The only person in Wichita Springs who would ever think of that."

Another woman, Sue, slid into one of the chairs at the table after listening to their conversation. "Sounds like there are only two of those wretched things. I saw them dragging the bodies back to the mine when I came here. I don't know what for. Maybe they're planning on... eating them... or something," she muttered, folding her hands together before bringing them to her face as if in prayer.

Sue had lived near Mitch and his mother since he could remember. His thoughts drifted to his mother and what could have only been horrific and agonizing final moments for her.

"Well, whatever is happening, it's got something to do with that mine," Betty replied. "People are saying the guys haven't been back from the mine in a couple days. No one's seen 'em."

Olive's ears perked, and she straightened attentively. "My dad works in the mine. Gareth Hayes." She looked at Mitch hopefully. "What if he's there? What if he's hurt and needs our help? We have to go to him!"

The creatures' otherworldly screams interrupted her. They were still far away, but there was no mistaking that they were headed in the direction of Mindy's.

Mitch saw the color drain from Olive's face, and he put his arm around her. "Hey," he said softly. "It's going to be okay. We'll figure it out." Looking at Mindy, Mitch called out, "We need to reinforce the windows and doors. Pile up anything you can find, and let's try to make some kind of blockade."

"Great idea, Mitchell," Mindy replied. She was smiling, but Mitch could tell she was nervous. "Alright, folks. Let's get moving!"

Within seconds, everyone was grabbing what they could—shelving, tables, chairs—and shoving the items against doors and windows. After a solid hour of hard work, Mindy's seemed to be decently fortified.

As the most able-bodied of the group, Mitch and Bill were given the guns and positioned themselves behind the cash register, ready to defend the remaining townsfolk from the demonic presence that was overtaking Wichita Springs.

Mindy handed glass bottles of alcohol, shredded souvenir t-shirts, and lighters to some of the adults to prepare Molotov cocktails.

Olive went to the largest window in the general store side of Mindy's and peered through the makeshift barrier. The ash falling from the sky floated delicately to the ground like snowflakes, but instead of a cozy Christmas white, the ash painted the landscape in a bleak, apocalyptic gray.

Distant movement caught her attention, past the trailer homes leading to the lake. Two spindly creatures were fighting over a body. One finally struck the other so hard that it skidded along the frozen surface of the lake, eventually rising to a crouching position and shaking its head before sullenly skulking away. The other ghoul watched the weaker one retreat, then began to drag the body toward the direction of the mine.

Her pulse raced as she imagined her father at the mercy

of the creatures, and she backed away from the window into Mitch who had been standing behind her.

"They're out there."

"Outside Mindy's?"

"Further off. Near the mine," Olive clarified.

She turned away, but Mitch reached for her and pulled her to him, embracing her tightly. "It'll be okay, Olivia. I promise."

***

After a while of sitting in tense anticipation, people began to grow weary and restless. Bill stood up from behind the register and stretched.

"Maybe they aren't coming back," Sue offered. "Maybe they had enough and will move on. Like animals who've had their fill."

Those near her visibly grimaced.

"We ain't dealin' with wolves here," one person retorted, his tone condescending.

All of a sudden, a scratching noise jolted the patrons of Mindy's from their debate.

Everyone tried to pinpoint where the noise had come from, and some were studying the ceiling.

Mitch put a finger to his lips and signaled to the others that something was on the roof. He knew it was one of the creatures probing for new ways into the diner.

"Is it Santa?" a child asked his mother.

She quickly placed a hand over the boy's mouth and looked at the others apologetically.

But it was too late. The monster had heard him. It let out a screech which was answered by the same cry from a distance.

"They're communicating," Olive told Mitch.

A single pound on the doors rattled the store. Seconds later, the pounding was joined by scratching and booming, almost as if the creatures were taking turns throwing themselves fully into the doors.

"Get ready!" Mitch yelled, hoping the barricades could withstand the impact. He knew the glass wouldn't hold much longer.

As he predicted, the doors immediately shattered, and the cobbled-together barricade exploded out as the creatures propelled forward.

All at once, panic engulfed Mindy's. Mitch and Bill fired the hunting rifles as quickly as they could, but the creatures were fast and nearly impossible to hit. They hunkered low to the ground, evading the bullets as they sprang toward the survivors.

It took the monsters no time at all to wreak havoc, easily swiping and slicing their claws through sinews, muscles, and flesh.

Mitch stopped firing for the briefest of seconds, realizing that their sharp blows appeared to wound and not kill. Once they had disabled everyone in the diner, they would presumably bring them all to the mine.

He blinked twice and re-focused his aim. There was nothing else to think about, but this moment and the need to survive.

One of the things leapt across the counter that Mitch was behind, forcing him to duck and scramble backward to avoid being attacked. Bill's reaction time was slower than Mitch's, however, and the creature swung forward, cutting him across the face. The end of its claws caught on the skin of his left eye socket, tearing it all the way to his scalp.

Bill screamed and grabbed his face, just as the creature hoisted him into the air and dragged him across the counter.

Mitch quickly stood up and fired, hitting the thing multiple times. Aside from angering it further, the weapons seemed to have little effect.

Several of the survivors had fled the diner when the creatures began their assault. Fear was consuming the last remaining members of Wichita Springs, and as Mitch watched the demon drag Bill's writhing body away, he realized he was not immune to it.

"Now, Olive!" he shouted.

Fire erupted onto the creature, setting it ablaze. It shrieked in agony, releasing Bill, before hurling itself outside toward the lake.

Olive yelped in pride and reached for another cocktail, throwing it at the creature as it fled.

A muffled scream came from the kitchen. The second ghoul, perched on a table in the diner, watched its cohort escape for a moment before swiveling its head in the direction of the scream.

Olive hadn't noticed it, but Mitch did. And his stomach turned when he saw what exactly had captured the creature's attention.

Mindy was standing in the kitchen, holding a large butcher knife in both of her hands. Behind her were two children and their mother. The knife wobbled in her grasp as she shook in trepidation, but a hard look of determination was etched on her face.

The creature sank its torso lower toward the floor as it crawled on all fours to them. Tangled in its claws was hair and blood.

Was it smiling? As it crept closer to Mindy and the small family, the corners of its lipless mouth formed a sinister grin.

Mitch's rifle was a bolt action with the ammunition tube beneath the barrel. Even though he'd already fired his last round, he spun the rifle around and wielded it like a baton before jumping over the safety of the counter toward the monster.

Olive saw him disappear into the kitchen and grabbed the closest thing to her, a large, heavy flashlight, and ran after him.

Mitch yelled as the rifle came crashing down on the back of the demon. The creature whirled around just as he opened both arms and tackled it to the ground. It struggled against him as Olive brought the flashlight down on its head. The blow itself didn't seem to be more than a nuisance to the creature, but the moment her fingers slipped and turned the flashlight on by accident, the bright LED glow shining into its inhuman eyes, it began to shriek and flail.

Still atop the creature, Mitch noticed that there were raw, grotesque burns appearing on the monster's face, marking the area of the flashlight's beam.

All of a sudden, it made sense to him, why the power had been drained from Wichita Springs, why Mindy's had been the last place the creatures hunted.

"Olive! Do it again! They hate the light!" Mitch exclaimed excitedly.

Olive brought the flashlight closer to the creature, jabbing it against its skin as she screamed and laughed at the same time.

The creature roared in agony as its translucent flesh sizzled and smoked. It thrust its shoulder against the hard floor, dislocating it, then managed to slice upward with its claws.

Mitch's overjoyed expression vanished in an instant, and he fell backward, clutching his chest as blood seeped through his plaid shirt.

The monster turned to Olive and hissed, the frightening noise emanating from a black chasm within its maw.

Afraid, she edged back a few steps, still holding the flashlight. The creature thrust out its other arm.

Olive dropped the flashlight and stared blankly at the gash across her forearm, so deep that she could see the bone as blood poured forth.

Mindy started to rush forward with her knife to help her. Sensing it was outnumbered and wounded, the creature looked from Olive to Mitch, then buried its claws into Mitch's ankle and dragged him out of Mindy's before either woman could stop it.

The last thing Mitch remembered was the sensation of soft flakes of ash landing gently on his skin and Olive frantically screaming his name.

Then everything went black as he succumbed to inevitable darkness.

Chapter VII

THE VALLEY OF ASH AND SHADOWS

Ash piled up between Mitch's legs and flowed over onto his stomach and chest as he was towed along. His eyelids fluttered as he shifted in and out of consciousness.

The creature's claws sank deeper into his right calf, and Mitch's eyes flew open. He shouted in protest and groaned something unintelligible.

Mitch craned his neck forward with the little strength he had and tried to assess the damage to his body. The claw marks were so deep on his chest that he could see muscle fibers through the shredded plaid material.

He laid back, exhausted from even the slightest effort. He wondered if Olive had survived the onslaught at Mindy's. What if the creature had come back seeking revenge after Olive had attacked it with a Molotov cocktail? She was alone with no one to help her. He had to stay awake; he had to fight this thing with everything left in him.

No one was coming to save him. It was up to him and him alone to get out of this thing alive.

Mitch attempted to bend his body forward to release himself from the creature's grasp, but it was useless. The mere pressure against his wounds was excruciating, and he gasped for breath, the last of his remaining energy siphoned.

Don't give in, Mitch, a voice in his head demanded.

Straining to see around the monster, Mitch could make out the entrance of the mine, the darkness within it ominous and foreboding. He tried not to imagine the nightmarish, grisly fate awaiting him.

His vision blurred, and he drifted back into unconsciousness once more.

The severe pain from his festering wounds awakened him, but this time, there was no ash around him. Trembling, he reached up to tenderly examine the wound on his chest. It had stopped bleeding, but the edges were raw and mushy to the touch.

Everything was dark, but there was a dull reddish glow coming from the back of the cave. He could hear dripping water, and the ground felt damp and cold beneath his fingertips as he lay there helplessly.

A screech bounced off the walls of the cave, far away, but not unthreatening. Fear coursed through Mitch, providing him with a slight boost in energy. He sat up and scooted backward against the wall, anxiously turning from side to side.

He observed a round, reflective portal of sorts, like something out of a science fiction film, emitting the red glow.

Strange scuffling and moaning coupled with movement began to echo from all around him. His hand grazed something smooth and clammy, and when it moved, he scrambled away.

Remembering his cell phone was in his pocket, Mitch fished it out and pressed the home button. Incandescent white light radiated from the phone, and suddenly, Mitch's worst fears were realized.

Bodies, dozens of them, were scattered across the ground. Some of them groaned in agony, mercifully still alive, but others were mere husks... shells of what they'd once been. Their eye sockets were empty, their mouths permanently frozen in terror. Their corpses were covered in leathery skin, all moisture sucked from their bodies, and each one was unnaturally bent backward, arms and legs rigidly outstretched. They looked as if they had been dead for years, mummified somehow, but as Mitch leaned in for a closer look, he easily recognized them as many of the townsfolk of Wichita Springs.

Movement in his periphery forced him to look away from the dead around him. Mitch hastily hid his phone, not knowing what was headed in his direction, and edged closer to the ground. He tried to blend in with the others and lay still, not wanting to draw any attention to himself. Peering over the shoulder of one of the husks, Mitch's eyes went wide.

An apparition of shadows appeared from the portal, floating above the bodies. Its cloak of darkness prevented Mitch from seeing its features. It was not one of the creatures from before, of that he was sure. It made wet, wheezing sounds as it glided past, finally stopping and hovering over one of the living.

No.

It was Doc Burrough. He flailed and waved his arms, trying to swat the mysterious specter away while hollering at it furiously.

Something quickly scrambled across the bodies, a white blur, and Mitch noticed that it was one of the creatures he'd fought at Mindy's. It paused just as it reached Doc Burrough and seemed to look at the shadowed figure for approval. Then it raised its clawed appendage and raked it across the older man's face, stunning him. The creature backed away, just as Doc Burrough was thrust into the air and pressed up tightly against the shadow.

Mitch felt his blood run cold as he watched the shadowed devil envelop his friend and suck the life from him.

Impulsively, Mitch grabbed his phone and held it up high. Light spread toward the creature and its master. As soon as the beams hit them, both howled and turned to him, the latter tossing aside Doc Burrough's lifeless husk.

The hand holding the phone began to shake as Mitch saw the shadowed mass in its entirety.

It had two thin legs, and its face was narrow and skeletal with eyes that burned like glowing embers.

It pointed its bony hand in Mitch's direction. Like an obedient dog, the pale creature leapt at Mitch.

In his shock, he clumsily dropped the phone. Mitch shifted about urgently trying to find it, ignoring the pain that seared through his body, knowing that without the light, he had nothing.

The brutal sensation of the flesh from his hamstrings ripping apart was the tell-tale sign they had reached him.

He slumped to the ground weakly. Seconds later, he felt something sharp flipping him over. Opening his eyes, Mitch found himself face to face with the dark skeletal creature sheathed in shadows.

The burning red eyes glared at him, and it lifted Mitch into the air, bringing its mouth close to his.

Mitch moved his arms futilely, but his body was damaged beyond repair.

Heavy jaws clamped down over his face. Almost

instantaneously, his flesh seemed to shrivel along his bones.

Mitch shut his eyes. This was it.

Goodbye, Mom.

Goodbye, Olive.

Suddenly, he was falling to the ground, landing against bodies that cushioned him from the cold, hard surface.

The soul-sucking ghoul was shrieking and retreated back into the portal.

Mitch slowly turned his head.

A glorious angel bathed in splendent light stood before him.

It was Olive, and she was covered in Christmas lights.

He had never seen anything so beautiful in his whole damned life.

When she was satisfied that the monsters were no longer a threat, she crouched down to Mitch.

"Hey," she said softly. Her eyes were sympathetic and full of concern. "You don't look so hot."

"Well, you have to be the best Christmas present a guy could ever ask for," he replied hoarsely.

She smiled, trying to help him to his feet. "You like this look, eh? Battery-powered Christmas lights, courtesy of Mindy."

Mitch was proud of her. "You're brilliant."

But then she noticed the mass of bodies that lay before them.

She clasped her hand over her mouth and fell to her knees, the crushing reality that her father could no longer be alive hitting her.

"Olive..." Mitch murmured, resting a hand on her shoulder. He wanted to console her, but they didn't have the luxury of time on their side. "We can't let this spread to another town. Whatever this is, it has to end here."

Olive shakily rose to her feet and tilted her chin up, trying to be brave. "There were sticks of dynamite near the entrance of the mine."

Mitch thought for a second. "That should be enough to close the portal."

"I'll go back and get them. Stay here." She started to unwind the Christmas lights from her body to give them to Mitch.

He held his hands out to stop her, wincing from the effort. "No, you keep them on."

"You can barely walk. You need the extra protection." She ignored him and wrapped them around his torso. "Just make sure this button stays on."

Mitch scowled at her. "What will you use if you run

into one of them?"

"I'll be fine." She tapped the flashlight against her palm and turned around, sprinting into a run.

When she returned a few minutes later, she held up several sticks of dynamite triumphantly. "Now we just need a lighter."

Mitch reached into his pocket.

"No way," she whispered disbelievingly.

He chuckled. "My dad gave it to me before he passed. It's one of the only things I have left from him. I rarely use it, but I always have it with me. Guess Dad saved the day even from the grave." He took the dynamite sticks from her and examined them. Frowning, he asked, "Was this all of it?"

Olive seemed puzzled. "That's everything. What's the problem?"

He pointed to the fuses. "The fuses aren't long enough. Usually they're five times this length at least. With them being this short…"

Her eyes widened in understanding. "We won't have enough time to run."

"Yeah," he replied. Mitch rubbed his hand over his face and leaned against the cave wall. He looked around, then settled his gaze on Olive. "Alright, give me the dynamite."

Olive shook her head defiantly. "No."

"I want you to run out of here as fast as you can."

"Not without you."

"Olive, everything I've ever known was in this town. You're the last person I care about, and I'm not going to let them take you, too."

"No, Mitch. You can't do this alone."

"Look at me, Olive. I'm not going to make it out of here, but you can." He straightened and took her hands in his. "And I'd like you to promise me something. Don't go backward. You're going to leave this mine, this town, and you're going to make a life for yourself—a good life—and you're going to find people who will support you and love you."

She pulled her hand from his to wipe away the tears as they streamed down her cheeks. "Mitch…" she started.

"Just promise me you'll do that, that you'll leave this place and go somewhere incredible. I hear New York is great this time of year."

She nodded. "Okay. I promise."

He wrapped her in his arms and pressed his lips against hers. "I'm gonna miss you, Olivia."

Then he stepped away from her and pocketed the sticks of dynamite except for one.

As he walked deeper into the mine, he paused momentarily. "One last thing... why did you come back for me?"

She looked him squarely in the eyes. "You're important to me."

Mitch smiled sadly, remembering his own words to her before.

Olive watched him stumble away, until the glowing lights fastened to his body were swallowed up by the darkness.

***

When Mitch returned to the dark recesses of the mine, there seemed to be more creatures coming through the portal, as if in desperation to stop him. They circled him, but from a distance, their expressions full of hatred. Occasionally, one or two would take a swipe at him, but instantly withdrew in pain when the lights strapped to him would sear their pale skin.

He inched forward a bit more.

The portal was almost liquid in its appearance, ripples vibrating along its surface. Mitch reached out to touch it, but first cast a quick glance over his shoulder to be sure nothing was going to ambush him.

Satisfied that they would leave him alone as long as the lights stayed on, he brushed his fingers along the exterior of the portal. For a brief moment, he ignored his pain and his mission as he capitulated to the fascination growing within him.

He had to see.

Just one look.

He pushed his head through the portal, but when he did, he immediately wished he hadn't.

A giant horned creature with white fur dropped what it was eating and stared at him with blood-red eyes. Mitch jerked his head back and retreated, his heart thumping wildly just as the Christmas lights began to flicker.

He reached into his pocket and grabbed the lighter, his other hand holding one of the sticks of dynamite.

The Christmas lights went out completely.

Mitch hastily thumbed the lighter, cursing when he only saw sparks.

He felt something slice into his calf muscle, and he shouted, dropping the dynamite just as the lighter emitted a small flame.

Mitch was being dragged away from the portal, back into the depths of the mine. He gritted his teeth, trying to find another stick of dynamite, but realized he'd lost them all when he fell.

He held out the lighter in front of him, screaming in agony as the creatures tore away at his legs.

A stick of dynamite had rolled into a crevice against the rock wall. It was a couple feet away next to the portal and out of arm's reach, but it was his only hope.

With one last heave, he clawed his way forward, just as the creatures ripped off what remained of his mutilated legs.

His fingers made purchase on the dynamite, and he touched the fuse to the lighter. He pulled himself up to the portal just as the dynamite exploded in his hands, bringing hell and all its angels down with him.

Epilogue

THE VALLEY OF ASH AND SHADOWS

December 25th, Christmas morning

Olive ran her fingertips over the smooth, glossy finish of the photograph in her hand, the one she'd retrieved from Luella's trailer, the one of Mitch with his parents in New York City.

After the explosion, she had returned to her father's trailer to pack her belongings. Inside her suitcase, hidden under her clothes, she'd found an olive jar covered in snowflake wrapping paper with a blue bow on the lid.

It was filled with ten thousand dollars in cash and a letter from her father. In it, he explained that he'd been setting aside money for her for a long time so that that she could put it toward whatever she needed to carve out a better life.

He also apologized for all of the pain he had caused her during her childhood, the years he missed being present as her father. It was his biggest regret, and he hoped the money would help make things right, and that she could find it in her heart to forgive him.

Reading it had been heartbreaking and cathartic all at once for Olive. The hole in her heart started to close, and she became more determined than ever to keep her promise to Mitch and to live a life that would make her father proud.

Olive hit the road, walking several miles to the Cherryton train station.

Whatever supernatural force holding the town captive had vanished. The crimson sky hanging over Wichita Springs became robin egg blue once more, and the dreadful falling ash was replaced with delightful, swirling snowflakes that coated her eyelashes.

She didn't bother to stick around for the investigation into the murders of the townsfolk of Wichita Springs. She knew law enforcement officials would never believe her story, that monsters had come through a portal inside of a mine to feed souls to an evil Grim Reaper of sorts. Even with the inexplicable falling ash and dark red sky indicating that something supernatural was at work, she would find her own story hard to believe, as well.

A train horn blared in the distance, shaking her from her reverie, and she lifted her head, feeling surprisingly at peace even though her life was about to drastically change.

The tracks at the station rattled and shook, pebbles bouncing along the wooden surface, as a train drew near.

It was Christmas morning, and people ambled closer to the platform, arms laden with beautifully wrapped packages and covered casseroles, eagerly chatting and laughing as they anticipated being with their families in nearby towns.

Olive felt a momentary pang of sadness that she was spending this Christmas alone. But Mitch's final words encouraged her. She would find people who would grow to love her.

She looked over her shoulder one last time at Wichita Springs in the distance before stepping onto the train. Smoke from the collapsed mine spiraled upward to the sky.

Wichita Springs had been the catalyst Olive needed to forge a new beginning, the opportunity to break free of a past riddled with addictions that nearly killed her, to rise from the ashes like a phoenix.

Olive had been fighting demons long before the creatures crawled out of the portal in the mine. She'd hit rock bottom already.

Things could only go up from here.

Chapter 7

Cora licked her lips. They felt cracked and dry, and she realized it had been several hours since she'd last had anything to drink. Her throat was raw, on fire, from talking so much. More than Damon liking her story, more than her freedom, what she wanted right now was a glass of water.

Damon looked as though he'd been crying. He stood, and when she saw the knife in his hand, she felt hopeful, thinking he was going to release her.

He liked the story! You'll be free!

"I have to kill you."

Wait. What?

No.

"I'm sorry." He took a step toward her, knife raised.

Cora pressed her back into the chair, recoiling from him. She shook her head fervently. "No, no. You can't! Please! If you kill me, you won't ever find out the code to the safe!" she cried in one last attempt to salvage her life. "Think about it—you would have more than enough to start over. You could leave this town and go anywhere, somewhere nice. Please…"

Damon paused.

Cora felt sweat dripping down her back, soaking her bra strap and trickling down to her pants.

Will he do it? Will he accept?

Much to her chagrin, he continued forward, and in one deft movement, the knife was pressed to her throat, cutting into her flesh slightly.

She had to act quickly.

Cora thrust up with her legs and struck him firmly in the groin with her knee, but the motion caused the chair to teeter backward. She hoped the wooden chair would shatter, just as it had in her stories, and she'd be free.

But instead, the chair hit the shelf behind her, knocking several items from it to the ground, before toppling over, and much to her disappointment, remaining fully intact. Her head roughly slammed against the wood floor.

Cora saw stars for a moment, and her vision blurred and then came back into focus just as Damon leaned down over her, his knife poised for her throat.

"Wait!" she croaked. "You don't have to do this! I know this isn't you."

He hovered just above her, so close that the knife blade

deflected the light into her eyes.

"You *don't* know me. But I know what *you've* been doing, weaving together stories to tug on my heartstrings. You're feeding me these salvation... *hero* stories that are... what... supposed to make me think twice about my life's decisions? It's a cheap trick. The first story was about siblings. You figured Marisa and I were close, that we loved each other." He shrugged and gestured to her body on the floor. "Well, evidently that wasn't the case. And then you tried to sell me on a story about two people in a bad marriage who end up saving it in the end. You took what I told you about my upbringing, the broken home, and you thought a happy mom and dad fairytale would appeal to me." He pointed the knife at her accusatorily. "And finally—and maybe worst—you tell me a story about a guy stuck in a shithole town, and he ends up doing the 'right thing' to save a girl he meets. Come on, Cora! I get it; they're all about me!"

Cora rolled her eyes. "If you think those stories were only about you, then your sister was right. You are an idiot."

Damon backed away a few inches, seemingly confused. "What are you talking about?"

"The stories. They were made for you, yes. To appeal to you, yes. But they weren't just about you."

"Who then? You? Your life has been perfect." His lip curled in disgust. "You'd say anything to not die."

"Every time a writer creates a story, little pieces of themselves are infused in them." She could see the turbulence in his eyes, the struggle between wondering what the hell she was going on about and knowing he could never let her live.

His curiosity won out, and he nodded at her to continue.

She lay there on the ground, her hands trapped beneath her, and stared up at the ceiling.

You don't want to do this. You don't want to go back there.

She took a steadying breath. "I have... had... a brother, a twin brother. We were always close, just like they say twins are. We could be in totally different places, but if something happened to him, I felt it, too." She remembered her brother when he was little, skinny legs and big, trusting brown eyes and curly brown hair. The sweetest, cutest kid in the world. "When we were in the sixth grade... some kid was bullying him everyday at the bus stop, and one time he beat up my brother bad, *really* bad. I was playing soccer after school, but I remember this awful feeling washing over me, like a literal pain in my stomach. When my mom picked me up from practice and told me the news, I already knew something had happened to him."

She squeezed her eyes shut.

Do you remember him? Do you remember how he

counted on you to protect him, to keep him safe?

Her brother's innocent smile flashed in her memory.

"So what happened to him?" Damon asked. He still stood over her with that stupid, shiny knife, but just as he was when she told the stories, he was rapt with interest once more.

"We attended all the same schools, had all the same teachers… But while he decided college wasn't for him and chose to stay in the town we grew up in, I wanted to go to a college far away from home. I wanted a sense of autonomy and independence, to figure out who I was as a person." That familiar pang of guilt jabbed at her insides. "At first, it was terrible. I didn't have my best friend. I felt lost. But then I started enjoying my freedom, got caught up in the parties, the late nights and endless weekends finishing papers and cramming for exams."

How did you just forget your brother? How could you do something like that?

"Like most girls in college, I got a boyfriend, and I spent most of my time with him. I'd never had a boyfriend before; it was exciting. I thought I loved him. I don't know why I chose my boyfriend over my brother, but however it happened, I stopped coming home to visit him."

Cora felt the tears roll down the sides of her face, into her hair. "One day, I was at my job waiting tables at this Italian restaurant. I remember I was holding a big tray full of plates of hot food, and I was carrying it to one of my tables. Suddenly I felt this horrible pain in my head, and I lost my balance and fell to the ground. I don't remember anything else except this huge red stain of spaghetti sauce on the carpet in front of me and all these broken plates everywhere." And still, now, she could see that dark crimson stain of spilled spaghetti sauce, how it widened across the floor, its symbolism haunting her, a permanent reminder of what happened on that wretched day. "I found out that my brother was killed in a car accident, hit by a drunk driver. His body was completely ejected out of the vehicle, and he hit a tree head first." She gasped suddenly. "They couldn't even have an open casket."

The truth of it was like a scorching pain, a vise-like grip that seared and squeezed her heart.

"The shittiest part of it wasn't that I never got the chance to say good-bye. It was that I never got to make it right with him, to apologize for not prioritizing him over the boyfriend who was an ex by the time senior year finished. The way we left our relationship, the way *I* left it, without salvaging it, without trying to restore it to how it was when we were kids… I have to live with that for the rest of my life."

"So those kids were supposed to be you and your brother."

"What I *wish* we could have been. But it's too late now, and no matter how deep I bury it, my past always finds a way to haunt me in my stories."

Chapter 8

"At least you had a sibling who loved you." Damon glanced at Marisa's body. When he looked back at Cora, his expression had changed, softened.

He went to her, and she cringed, shutting her eyes, knowing her time had finally run out.

But then he moved behind her, grabbing the chair and placing it upright so that she was no longer laying on the floor.

"What about the next one, with the couple on the brink of divorce?"

Cora winced, another painful remembrance forced to the forefront of her memory. "I was married once. To an incredible, loving, loyal man. And somehow I managed to screw that up, too. Instead of being a wife to him, a partner, all I did was write, day in and day out. When I hit *The New York Times* bestsellers list, it went to my head. I admit it, it totally did. And eventually, I started to think I was better than him, that I could get better. He was just a run-of-the-mill high school teacher after all, and here I was, this hot-shot writer."

Damon sat down across from her.

Cora's breath caught in her throat as she tried to hold back a sob. "I met someone. At a writers' convention. He was a publicist. It was instant chemistry. That night, I had one too many drinks at the hotel bar where we were both staying. My husband was home. He couldn't attend the convention with me because his students were in finals. I was bitter about it, stupidly so. I wanted him to drop everything to support my ambitions. This guy and I started taking shots, and the next thing I remember was waking up naked beside him in his room." Her chin drooped to her chest. "I swore it wouldn't happen again, but I wanted more, and I was ruthlessly ambitious. The publicist could get me more exposure, better deals. So the affair continued. It didn't take long for my husband to put two and two together. He knew something was wrong. I was cold and distant. I barely touched him. Eventually, he found the texts, went through the call history. He confronted me, and when I admitted the affair, the next day he went out and filed for divorce."

Snot dribbled from her nose. "I remember as a kid how much I wanted a happy marriage, how much I dreamed about it. Like your mother. I was one of those little girls who loved dressing up in her mom's old wedding gown." She managed to smile sadly at the memory. Little Cora. Pure as the freshly fallen snow outside and still untainted by greed and selfishness. "I remember the look on my husband's face when I confessed, the utter betrayal in his eyes. It was like he wanted me to prove him wrong, that those texts and calls were just in his imagination. I know I broke him. I know I took his heart and stomped on it, and maybe I've ruined his ability to ever really love someone wholly again."

She wondered how he was, if he had forgiven her. But in his shoes, Cora wouldn't have forgiven her crimes. "It didn't take me long to realize I'd made a terrible mistake. I found out the publicist was screwing around with lots of women, not just me. I tried to reconcile with my husband, but it was too late. When I showed up at his friend's house where he'd been staying until everything was finalized with the divorce, I begged him for another shot. But there was nothing I could do at that point. He hated me. I'd lost my chance forever."

Damon seemed oddly satisfied with her explanations. "I guess you're not such a perfect angel after all."

Almost more than being restrained, more than knowing her life would surely end at any moment, it hurt the most to dig up all of the painful memories she had suppressed for so long in her heart, the ones she wished would vanish... the mistakes, the sins...

He stared at her long and hard. "Why did you think I was Mitch?"

"What?" She blinked rapidly, bewildered.

"What did you mean by it? That I'd sacrifice myself somehow to save you?"

Cora shook her head. "Mitch... he's not you."

"But everything about him had me written all over it."

"No."

"Mitch wants something bigger, better."

She felt anger building up inside of her.

He's toying with you. He never intended to let you go. You're tied up like some kind of roast pig, emptying your closet full of skeletons to him for his amusement.

It's pathetic how you trusted him, a complete stranger, how you put it all out there, those stories about yourself. It's always been the two of us. He's going to kill you. You'll never get out of this. You've failed your brother, your husband... and now you've failed yourself.

"Shut up already!" Cora shouted.

Damon looked around the room, then tilted his head at her. "Ummm... I didn't say anything." A peculiar look was on his face.

The voice in her head silenced. "People say talking about your past gives you closure," she continued. "It doesn't. It only makes you realize you can never go back and change it for the better." Cora couldn't handle anymore. If he didn't kill her, she might just do it for him. "My point is, you're not the only one with baggage. No more stories, Damon. If you're going to kill me, just do it already. I'm done," she whispered firmly.

Damon was silent for several minutes. "You're going to give me the code to the safe. And…"

Cora didn't look up at him. She couldn't.

"And I'm going to cut you free. No more stories. You've kept up your end of the deal, and now I'll keep mine."

Her head jerked up in surprise. "You're setting me free?"

He stood, the knife open in his hand.

Instead of slicing her open the same way he did Marisa, Damon knelt down behind her.

"What's the code?"

"How do I know you're telling the truth? That you won't just kill me as soon as I give it to you?"

"You don't," he said softly. "I guess you'll just have to trust me."

Cora swallowed hard, like she was trying to digest a wad of cotton, and somehow it had lodged itself in her throat.

Damon sighed, feigning impatience, but Cora could see the anticipation glittering in his eyes, the eagerness of discovering the unknown treasure waiting for him in the safe, something even better than the bars of gold.

"Five-four-one-two," she stammered.

As promised, he started cutting the ropes that held her captive. As soon as they gave way, she got up and retreated slowly, massaging her wrists where they'd been rubbed raw from her restraints.

Damon observed her intently, but folded his knife and tucked it into his pocket. "First you're going to show me where the safe is, then you can scram."

"It's in the bedroom, behind the painting on the wall."

Damon rose and looked at the bedroom, then back at her, trying to assess if she was telling the truth. But his eyes were no longer brooding and angry. They held an understanding, a familiarity, a kindred state of spirits.

"I'm sorry it happened this way." Then he turned and walked into the bedroom.

Cora's gaze shifted back and forth between the bedroom and the door leading to the garage.

The corner of her laptop poked out from Marisa's duffel bag, a reminder of what was still undone.

Do it.

***

The painting above Cora's dresser was now sitting at an angle on the floor. Damon cursed under his breath as he tried repeatedly to correctly turn the dial on the safe. He couldn't remember… was it three rotations to the right, then one to the left, then one to the right again? The last time he'd fumbled around with a dial similar to this had been in high school with his locker.

Finally, he heard the safe click, and with a tentative, curious hand, he opened the door.

His eyes narrowed in confusion.

This wasn't what he expected.

It was an assortment of random objects.

A letter opener.

A hammer.

A serving fork.

Things that had no business being in a safe.

He didn't notice them though; what he saw was something shiny peeking through the worthless, puzzling items, and he sifted around, wondering what prize would be obscured beneath them.

It was another bar of gold.

At least his efforts hadn't been for nothing.

But then he saw something on the gold, something that dulled its brilliance.

On one corner of the bar was dried blood.

Clumps of tattered old hair.

"What…?" he murmured as he removed the brown

strands from the gold.

That was when he focused his attention on the other objects. His hands now trembling, he examined each one, seeing shriveled chunks of an unknown substance and more blood… on the end of the hammer, along the prongs of the fork, coating the entirety of the letter opener.

But before he could say anything else, before he could turn around, something punctured his neck, easily tearing apart sinewy muscle like butter. He stumbled back until he was face to face with Cora, in her hand the antique pen that had once decorated her beloved bookshelf.

Chapter 9

"I didn't just want to be a writer."

Cora lifted the pen to her nose, inhaling the coppery scent of blood with pleasure.

"Like Mitch, I wanted something bigger and better. I wanted everyone to know my name. I wanted to make every bestseller list. I wanted to be the best."

You are the best, Cora.

Her eyes were cold, unfeeling. "But I guess at the end of the day, I wasn't actually anything like Mitch. I don't care what I have to do to get inspiration, whatever I need to do to take my book from *meh* to *can't-put-it-down*."

Cora's phone rang unexpectedly from the kitchen, its chirping, cheerful ringtone starkly out of place amidst the carnage. She pulled away from Damon. It was the ringtone for her agent.

She looked at the bloody pen in her hand and then methodically placed it inside the safe beside the hammer, the fork, the bar of gold, and the letter opener.

After closing the door to the safe, Cora rehung the painting and sauntered into the kitchen. She took a napkin and wiped away some of the still-wet blood from her hand. Taking the cell phone from the counter, she slid her finger across the screen and turned on the speaker while she stared at Marisa's body on the floor.

"Was this you?"

There was a long pause. *"What do you think?"* a male voice answered.

Cora scoffed. "You idiot! You could have killed me."

The man chuckled. *"You're like a cockroach. Even the apocalypse won't kill you. And besides, you were struggling to find motivation. I just wrapped it up nice and neat and placed it on your doorstep."*

"What do you mean?"

"Word travels fast in these parts. I just had to whisper in the right ears that a rich writer lived on this mountain. Those two losers were practically salivating when I told them what was at stake."

"I could have been killed. He almost slit my throat."

"I knew you'd be fine. You're not exactly a shrinking violet when it comes to this shit."

Cora was livid. "How did you know they wouldn't kill me?"

"I didn't. But I know you, and I know what you're capable of."

"'What I'm capable of?'"

Again, he chuckled. *"It wouldn't be the first time you needed macabre inspiration."*

"Go to hell, Patrick. It's not funny."

"Come on; we're both going to benefit from this."

Cora froze, her brain laser-focused and electric with... something.

She quickly squatted down next to the bag on the ground beside Marisa. When she found her laptop, she pulled it out and set it on her desk.

"Are you seriously mad at me, Cora?"

She ignored him and plugged the power adapter into the port on the side.

"Cora?"

"I'll call you later. Clean this mess up, Patrick. I need to write."

The screen whirred to life, too slow for her liking. Her fingers twitched centimeters above the keyboard, itching to type.

She pulled up the last manuscript she'd been working on and began clicking away on the keys, smearing blood across them unintentionally, but not caring in the slightest.

Cora's lips turned up subtly at the corners.

Her well was replenished; she was inspired once more.

But for how long?

About the Authors

Angelique Archer and J. Mills live in the D.C. area and met during a murder trial. In 2018, they tied the knot and have been crime fighters ever since! As part of an annual tradition, Angelique and her husband craft short stories for limited-edition anthologies in partnership with other renowned authors, and this year they decided to weave them together into a full-length standalone thriller.

Angelique and her husband enjoy traveling and exploring the world together, spending time with family and friends, camping, brainstorming solid story/movie ideas, hanging out with their awesome cat, Taco, and their three flying squirrels, and watching movies while eating pizza.

Keep in touch with Angelique at:

angelique.archer.author@gmail.com

Follow her on Facebook and Amazon Author Central:

bit.ly/AngeliqueArcher-Author

Amazon.com/author/angeliquearcher

Made in the USA
Middletown, DE
16 September 2025

13419085R00170